Six . . .

Six skeleto...

Plain Jane Kurtz is going to use her winnings to discover her inner vixen.
But what's it *really* going to cost her?

New girl in town Nicole Reavis is on a journey to find herself. But what *else* will she discover along the way?

Risk taker Eve Best is on the verge of having everything she's ever wanted.
But can she take it?

Young, cocky Zach Haas loves his instant popularity, especially with the women.
But can he trust it?

Solid, dependable Cole Crawford is ready to shake things up.
But how "shook up" is he prepared to handle?

Wild child Liza Skinner has always just wanted to belong.
But how far is she willing to go to get it?

Million Dollar Secrets—do *you* feel lucky?

Blaze™

Dear Reader,

When I was asked to write a novel for the
MILLION DOLLAR SECRETS continuity series,
I was thrilled. For years I've been contributing to
my office lottery pool and have often dreamed of
winning it big with my friends and coworkers. But
I've also read enough real-life stories to know that
winning a fortune doesn't always bring happiness.

That's what Nicole Reavis discovers when her
lottery win brings more headaches than wealth,
plus a slew of publicity when she moves to Atlanta
seeking peace. Of course, when all's said and done,
she finds her peace thanks to a love that money
can't buy.

I hope you enjoy this continuation of the
MILLION DOLLAR SECRETS series. Please
drop me a note and tell me what you think of it.
You can contact me through my Web site at
www.LoriBorrill.com or mail me in care of Harlequin
Books, 225 Duncan Mill Road, Don Mills, Ontario
M3B 3K9, Canada.

Happy reading!

Lori Borrill

UNDERNEATH IT ALL
Lori Borrill

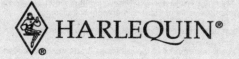

TORONTO • NEW YORK • LONDON
AMSTERDAM • PARIS • SYDNEY • HAMBURG
STOCKHOLM • ATHENS • TOKYO • MILAN • MADRID
PRAGUE • WARSAW • BUDAPEST • AUCKLAND

ISBN-13: 978-0-373-79348-8
ISBN-10:   0-373-79348-0

UNDERNEATH IT ALL

ABOUT THE AUTHOR

An Oregon native, Lori Borrill moved to the Bay Area just out of high school and has been a Californian ever since. She credits her writing career to the unending help and support she receives from her husband and real-life hero. When not sitting in front of a computer, she can usually be found at the Little League fields playing proud parent to their son, Tom. She'd love to hear from readers and can be reached through her Web site at www.LoriBorrill.com.

Books by Lori Borrill

HARLEQUIN BLAZE
308—PRIVATE CONFESSIONS

Many thanks to Kathryn Lye for giving me the opportunity to work on this project and having faith that I could do it.

And thanks to Leeanne Kenedy for giving me the support and encouragement I needed to see this project through. I can't wait to return the favor!

This book is for Al and Tommy, my forever and always.

1

"OKAY, LADIES, THE NEXT man up for grabs is Evan Phillips, this handsome real estate broker for Century South." The woman at the microphone motioned to the dark-eyed hunk on stage and added, "Evan, please tell the women in the crowd what they're bidding on."

While the man detailed a romantic evening starting with dinner at Atlanta's infamous Sun Dial restaurant, Nicole Reavis turned to her friend and coworker, Eve Best. "Some days I love my job."

Eve smiled. "As opposed to days when you're stuck in a catfight between girlfriends?"

Nicole winced. As chief segment producer for Eve's cable talk show, *Just Between Us,* much of her job involved researching topics for upcoming shows. Tonight, it was the annual Children's Charities Bachelor Auction, a glamorous event at a trendy new club where some of the city's most eligible bachelors auction off a night on the town for charity.

Three days ago, the job had her dodging blows between two women who'd claimed to get along beautifully even though they were both dating the same man.

Proof that in the world of daytime television, life was never dull.

"And *I* noticed you've come here tonight but were conveniently AWOL when I was screaming for security before those women destroyed our conference room." Nicole shook her head. "Thank heavens we got them together *before* we put them on the air. How humiliating would that have been?"

"Hey, if I'd been there you know I would have jumped in and helped."

Nicole smiled in agreement, knowing Eve would have come running if she'd been in the studio at the time. Though Nicole was the new girl on the set, she and Eve had hit it off right from the start. She'd hit it off with everyone on the crew, for that matter, and the catfight incident was quickly becoming known as Nicole's official transformation from newbie into battle-scarred veteran.

"Besides, I needed to be here tonight to help make sure Penny doesn't get herself into trouble." Eve scanned the large crowd. "Where is she, by the way?"

Penny was one of Nicole's new research assistants, a young woman just out of college, barely of legal drinking age, and highly naive, almost too much so for a talk show that focused on relationships and sex. But the eighteen to twenty-five demographic was a hot one, and Nicole was willing to overlook Penny's inexperience for the perspective she brought to the show.

"She's getting the list of participants from the organizers. It'll be interesting to interview them after their dates to see how this sort of thing generally turns out for couples."

"We'll start the bidding at two hundred dollars," the woman onstage said.

The announcement caused a swarm of hands to go up. It looked as though the sexy real estate broker would be a hot commodity this evening.

Admittedly, before she came here tonight, Nicole had faced the evening with skepticism, wondering why this group of obviously successful singles would pay such a high price for what equated to a blind date. Surely, they couldn't expect to find their soul mates under circumstances like this.

But once inside the doors, she realized this wasn't about finding soul mates, it was about fun and fantasy, and the organizers of this event had played every angle to that end. Every year, the auction was held at one of Atlanta's swankiest new spots, tonight's at a bar called Oasis. The place was high class all the way, the interiors alone surely costing the owners a small fortune.

Set up like an underwater tide pool, the walls were painted in murals that gave the feeling one was standing on the ocean floor. Art glass chandeliers hung overhead like floating squids and sea urchins, glass seashells adorned the sconces that lined the perimeter. The floor was tiled to look like sand with touches of mother of pearl embedded here and there, and the moment Nicole had stepped inside, she was swept into the surreal atmosphere.

The place was like entering the soothing realm of an underwater aquarium, deep and mysterious, the ideal canvas for the sensual prospects of what might come.

And then, of course, there was the man across the room. The one she'd been trying to ignore all evening without any success. Not that she had an aversion to sinfully gorgeous men. On the contrary, she happened to like them a lot, and this one in particular kept pulling her attention toward him like a magnet on steel.

That was the problem. She was supposed to be observing the crowd, selecting couples of interest and taking notes for the show, and she was having trouble doing that with Mr. Delicious over there tossing her thoughts between the sheets.

She was a sucker for a man in a suit, and the charcoal gray classic he wore did wonders for a body that probably didn't need the help. The silvery blue tie matched his eyes, bringing them to life even under the dim lighting of the undersea bar. But it was his smile that did the most damage, the kind that could bring a woman to her knees: gentle but teasing, with a faint dimple on one cheek to temper his strong jaw. His dark hair was cut short and brushed back in a style reminiscent of James Dean's rebel days.

He stood relaxed and casual, as though the suit he wore was as comfortable as a pair of old blue jeans, and he had a laugh that seemed to come from the heart. Everything about the man felt genuine, as if he was oblivious to his own appeal. There was nothing pretentious or calculating in his eyes as they scanned his surroundings, and the more Nicole watched him, the more she felt like she could stand and stare all day.

A sharp knock of the gavel brought her back to attention a moment too late, and she cursed under her breath. This was now the third couple she'd missed by ogling Mr. Delicious, and with a self-deprecating frown she turned to Eve and asked, "How much did that one go for?"

Eve chuckled. "What's with you tonight? Too many sexy men putting you on overload?"

"No, just one," she said, moving her gaze back to places it didn't belong.

Eve followed her line of sight. "Which one?"

"The tall one in the middle," Nicole said absently.

"What tall one, what am I missing?"

The question came from Penny who'd just returned with the list from the charity's organizer.

"Nicole's found a man to bid on tonight," said Eve.

"What? No, I haven't," Nicole said. "I just find him attractive, that's all." Though increasingly, the thought of him being taken by another woman tonight brought her an uneasy pang of jealousy she didn't quite understand.

Again her traitorous eyes wandered over in his direction. For nearly an hour, he'd been standing there, one hand in his pants pocket, gracefully pulling back the suit jacket to offer a peek of what looked like the rigid lines of a well-toned chest and abs. And for nearly an hour, Nicole had been trying to keep her mind on the job and off the tall stallion in the corner, but it was becoming increasingly difficult.

He took another sip of his drink and moved his eyes across the room as the man standing next to him continued to fill his ear with conversation. Mr. Delicious had one ear to the conversation while he masterfully surveyed his surroundings. Nicole suspected these types of affairs, this mingling of business and pleasure were a common occurrence for him, and she wondered who he was and what he did for a living.

Once again, the man laughed, the sound reverberating through her veins and numbing her fingers, and just when she felt she should really look away, his gaze swept back over the room and landed directly on her.

Those crystal blue eyes clicked squarely with hers, growing in intensity as she noted the faint rise of interest in his brow. That soulful mouth she'd just been admiring twitched and smiled, leaving her feeling aroused and exposed.

Was she hot from lust or the embarrassment of being caught ogling? And if it was the heat of embarrassment, why couldn't she find the will to dart her eyes away?

His simple glance paralyzed her, freezing every bone in her body to the point where she couldn't even blink. And when he brushed his gaze down her body, it was as though a thousand fingers moved with it, touching every sensitive spot on the way.

That a simple look could heighten so many nerve endings left her anticipating what he could do with the extra sense of touch. Given the way she felt right now, she almost didn't want to find out. If there really was such a thing as spontaneous human combustion, this man had the power to unleash it.

"Oh, if that's not an invite, I don't know what is," Penny said.

It was the jab to the ribs more than the comment that brought Nicole's attention back to the conversation at hand.

She cleared her throat and spun around, feeling ridiculous that for the fourth time tonight, the man in the corner managed to derail her thoughts. Maybe everyone was right that she'd been working too hard in light of the recent fiasco they'd all been thrown into.

As if her life hadn't been complicated enough, Nicole and the crew of *Just Between Us* had recently won Lot'O'Bucks, the state's biggest lottery. The one-in-a-gazillion shot had transformed the five of them from average working class to multi-millionaires overnight.

For Nicole, the win had been a sign that her move to Atlanta had been the right thing to do. Up until then, she hadn't convinced herself that leaving her home and a promising career back in California had been the smartest decision. At the time, she'd been reeling from the news that her life had been a lie, that she wasn't the person she thought she was, and that her real roots hadn't even been in California.

She was actually a native Southern girl, and like an immigrant looking to make her way back home, she'd come to Atlanta to try and sort through the clutter that had become her life. She'd taken a step down in her career, seeking out the small cable show believing the slower pace would give her time for reflection.

Unfortunately, the job proved to be more demanding and hectic than she'd expected. She hadn't had time to think, much less reflect on where she belonged in this world. She'd become uncertain, a little homesick, and began doubting her move to Georgia. Until the lottery win that changed their lives and her perspective on everything.

Nicole had taken it as Fate assuring her that though this path might be rocky, she was on the right road, and despite the media frenzy the win propelled them into, it had given her a sense of comfort that she'd been longing for.

Until Liza and her lawsuit.

Liza Skinner was Nicole's predecessor on the show and one of the founding members of *Just Between Us*. She and the other four lottery winners, Cole, Jane, Zach and Eve, had been playing Lot'O'Bucks since they started the show three years ago. But when Liza took off without a word, the group needed to replace her, and with Nicole coming in to fill her position at the station, she thought she'd go the distance and take her place in the lottery pool as well.

At just a few dollars a month, Nicole figured, why not? And when they won, leaving them all to split thirty-eight million dollars after taxes, she was happy she had.

Unfortunately, a win this big made national headlines and drew Liza Skinner out of the woodwork. She hadn't wasted time coming back to Atlanta to claim her portion of the prize, and though the group hadn't felt she was owed any part of it, apparently Liza's lawyer disagreed. Since then, their winnings had been on hold, everyone's plans suspended, and Nicole had gone back to wondering whether or not the South was really meant for her after all.

Surely, all these things coming to a head were simply catching up with her tonight. Walking into this undersea garden and its atmosphere of sex and romance, she was simply letting the strain of the last several months carry her away.

That's all it was.

Right?

She looked into Penny's evil wide-eyed gaze. "You should bid on him."

Nicole attempted to act as though that were the most ridiculous thing she'd heard, but even she could feel the weakness in the effort.

"I'm not bidding on anyone," she replied, not sounding the least bit convincing.

"Come on. We're researching this auction for the show. What better way to gain insight than to play along."

Nicole glanced at Eve, who actually seemed to be going along with Penny's crazy idea.

"She's got a point," Eve agreed.

Biting her lip, Nicole turned and eyed him once more. It was one thing to admire the man from afar. Heck, it would even be another to wander over and start a conversation. But to force him into a date by winning him in an auction? Could she really go that far?

Taking in another drink of the sexy stud, she wondered who she was kidding. Of course she could. In a heartbeat.

"You need to do this," Penny said. "For the show."

"For the show," Nicole repeated.

DEVON BRADSHAW SIPPED HIS bourbon while admiring the sweetest thing he'd seen since his mother's peach pie. Tall, blonde and beautiful, the woman had captured his eye with just a glance and gave him hope that this night might not end badly.

He and his brothers, Bryce and Todd, had been roped into this charity event by their sister, Grace. At the time, she claimed she hadn't realized it was a bachelor auction, and when offered the opportunity to back out, Bryce, the sensible one, did exactly that. Devon planned to follow until Todd challenged him. The one who goes for the highest bid wins, loser has to double the winner's bid for charity. Even then, Devon tried to weasel out of it until word of the challenge got back to Grace and the charity organizers and one thing led to another and…well…here he was, wondering what he'd end up with after the night was through.

All in all, it was good for business, just another stop in a string appearances aimed at keeping Bradshaw Investments in good corporate standing with the major money-handlers of Atlanta. As future CEO of the family business, functions like this had become one of his least favorite parts of the job.

But the stunning blonde across the room changed everything.

Slim, striking, fresh as a summer day, the woman had that special something that left him with hope. More fit and slender than plush and curvy, she had a runner's body and light caramel skin, the type who wouldn't look foreign in roller blades and jeans, but easily softened into a Southern belle in that pretty pink dress and heels.

He liked the contradiction, and as he continued watching her through the crowd, he wondered if the look in her eye meant this night might end on a high note.

"I can't believe you two are really doing this."

The whining voice of reason came from Bryce.

"Would you stop with the complaining already? Besides, I thought you'd enjoy spending the evening watching Todd's public humiliation."

"Neither of you should be humiliating yourselves at this auction. We should all be back at the office trying to figure out who's stealing money from the company."

Devon scoffed. "We don't know that there's any stealing going on, and if there is, we'll get the report from accounting once they pinpoint the discrepancies in the books."

"This is serious. We should be more hands-on about this."

There being the statement that reminded Devon on more than one occasion that Bryce should be the one inheriting the job as CEO of Bradshaw Investments. If their father had made the choice based on who was best suited, it would have been Bryce all along. The man had the eye for numbers and the wit for business that made him the natural choice. It was only birth order that put him in the position as head of finance instead.

According to their father, William Devon Bradshaw III, who inherited the family business from his
father, William Devon Bradshaw Jr., tradition had
it that the next logical CEO would be the next
William Devon Bradshaw. That had been the assumption from the day Devon was born, and every
step he'd taken in life had been leading toward that
end. He had a masters in economics and business
management, had been working with the firm since
his apprenticeship back as a teen.

It was all laid out for him, just as it had been laid
out for all the Bradshaws before him. The only
problem with the whole scenario was that he was
bored to death with the job, and he'd only now
come to the realization that life wouldn't get more
interesting the farther up the ladder he went.

Though technically still in charge, their father had
been slowly stepping back, letting Devon handle the
operation, and now that he'd finally had a glimpse
of the life he was to inherit, he didn't like what he
saw. This business of investments and numbers was
comatose at best, and increasingly, he doubted he
could last another year, much less the rest of his life.

The only question now was what to do about it.
Given their annual audit had uncovered suspicious
discrepancies in the books, now was not the time
to start the certain shake-up that would occur when
Devon announced he'd like to make a break from
tradition. When it came to investing, people were
nervous and image meant everything. If there was

anything shady going on within the company, they'd need to resolve that first and let the dust settle before dropping any more bombs.

And the announcement that a first-born Bradshaw had his own ideas about his future was certain to create some fall-out.

"I mean it," Bryce added under his breath. "We have to face the real prospect that someone's stealing from the company."

Devon slugged back the last of his drink, deciding the only prospect he cared to deal with tonight was the blonde across the room.

Slinging an arm around Bryce's shoulder, he led the man the few steps toward the bar. "Let me give you some brotherly advice. For the next few hours, forget about the audit. You're better off here exuding calm confidence than hovering over the accountants distracting them from their job. They've got your cell phone number and if something comes up, they'll call."

He ordered a drink and slid a twenty across the sleek marble bar.

"I see," Bryce said. "And while I'm forgetting about the audit, you'll be busy working the blonde over there."

He winked and smiled. "I like the way you think, bro."

Bryce frowned but didn't press. More than anyone, he knew Devon's heart wasn't in the family business. He only doubted Devon had the guts to admit it to their father. And who knows, maybe he didn't.

All he knew was that tonight he didn't want to think about futures or audits or career aspirations. There was an intriguing woman with sharp-witted blue eyes calling for his attention, and there was nothing in the auction's rule book that said he couldn't try to influence the buyers in any way.

He gestured to Bryce. "Who's that she's talking to? Don't we know her?"

Bryce eyed the shorter brunette from across the large room.

"You know who that is?" Bryce said. "I think that's the woman with that talk show. *Between Friends,* or *Our Time,* or something like that. I forget the name. It's kind of a chick show, but it's getting pretty popular."

"Oh, yeah. I know the one you're talking about." He picked up his drink and took a sip. "I wonder if the blonde works for the show."

"If she does she's a millionaire. You heard about that, didn't you?" When Devon shook his head, Bryce explained, "A bunch of them won Lot'O'Bucks. They're all millionaires—the brunette for sure." He added with a shrug, "Maybe they're here to spend their fortune."

"Deep pockets would certainly work in my favor." Setting his drink on the bar, he added, "I think I'll go introduce myself."

Bryce opened his mouth, no doubt to object, but

before he could speak a low voice behind them interrupted.

"Why, if it isn't my favorite investment broker. How much am I going to have to pay for you tonight?"

The cold chill told Devon it was Abigail Westlaw, a local real estate agent with whom he, in a temporary loss of sanity, had made the mistake of sleeping with. Once. Granted, it wasn't that he didn't find Abbey attractive enough to go back for seconds. A fair share of heat had simmered between them. The problem was that no sooner had they finished their morning coffee than Abbey was all over town spreading every detail of the tryst to anyone who would listen.

And thanks to that, out of the woodwork came a dozen other men who'd shared heat with Abbey, all interested in comparing notes.

Call him old fashioned, but Devon had never been interested in communal sex. He preferred being the one-and-only, and if he'd taken his time and gotten to know the woman better, he would have discovered before making the mistake that Abbey Westlaw liked her men frequent and interchangeable.

He forced a smile and replied, "Why bid on used goods? Surely, you'd be more interested in someone new and shiny."

Please?

She threw her head back in an overexaggerated laugh and slung a bony arm over his shoulder. "Devon, you were always the funny one."

The funny one?

Wincing, he tried to remain calm, remembering there were worse things than spending a romantic evening with Abbey. Though off the top of his head, he couldn't come up with any.

Abbey kissed him on the cheek and gave his arm a squeeze.

"If the price is right, I might go home with several prizes tonight," she said, her expression stating she had no clue as to how bad that sounded. "I just wanted you to know you're my first choice."

And with that, she walked off, leaving him standing at the bar with one sinking pit in his stomach.

2

"I HOPE YOU'VE COME prepared to lose," said Devon's brother, Todd. "I've got several women in this room ready to fork out big dollars for a slice of the best looking Bradshaw."

"I'm glad you've come with confidence," Devon replied half-heartedly. He wasn't terribly interested in engaging in another battle of egos with the baby of the family. Abbey's parting words were still hanging in his ears, leaving him thoroughly annoyed with his brother for talking him into this mess.

"It's not confidence, it's strategy," Todd said, pointing a finger to his forehead. "A good gambler knows the way to win is to tilt the odds in his favor. So while you were standing here holding hands with Bryce, I've been securing bidders." He scanned the room and smiled. "And I've got my odds set on a sexy redhead named Tammy."

Devon had to admit, before spotting the blonde he hadn't considered working the room, even though most of the men here tonight had been casually mingling through the crowd. He was still a little put off by the idea of auctioning himself off like a steer marked for stud. Playing along by actively promoting himself tipped the weird meter a bit too far.

But for Todd, this kind of thing was right up his alley. The born salesman of the three Bradshaw boys, Todd could talk a vagrant out of his last dollar and leave him sorry he couldn't give more. Add the heat of competition and the spark of a friendly wager and this night was Todd's all around, the kind of thing he was made for.

Their father hadn't been stupid to put Todd in charge of investor acquisitions at the firm. He loved talking people out of their money and though Devon often found his younger brother's ego tiresome, he had to admit Todd was good at his job.

Which was why Devon showed up tonight already accepting surrender. From the moment Todd could walk and talk the family learned not to go up against him when it came to competition. Even as kids at their old church fundraisers, if someone raised twenty dollars, Todd would work double-time to raise twenty-one. The little snot would do anything to win, and it was decades ago that Devon, Bryce and Gracie all learned it was easier to not compete than suffer through the lengths he'd go to come out on top.

But though Devon had no interest in trying to beat Todd tonight, he most certainly wanted to end up on a date with the only woman in the room who perked his interest—among other things.

Still talking among her friends, she'd turned around, giving him a glorious view of one heart-shaped behind, and he clenched his hands into fists as if to ward off the desire to walk over and caress them over her ass. Just that one heated glance they'd shared had left him feeling as though he had the right, as if he'd claimed her through the crowd, and he had to forcefully pull his civility back in check.

Like a caveman considering walking over and dragging her off to his cave, the woman had somehow reached in and yanked on his most primal instinct to conquer and possess, and before he approached her, he needed to remind himself that his species had supposedly evolved.

Right now, however, it didn't feel like it.

"How about you? You got any prospects lined up?" Todd asked.

"Abigail Westlaw," Bryce said with a smirk.

"Yeah, you and twenty others." Todd studied Devon as if he were sizing up the competition. "Really, no joke. You haven't talked to any women here tonight?"

"I was about to introduce myself to a lovely blonde," Devon said, moving his gaze back across the room.

"The blonde from *Just Between Us?*" Todd asked.

"You know her?" Devon asked, his interest in his brother piquing.

Todd glanced over to the blonde and the two

women she was with. "Know of her. She's one of the producers of the TV show. Eve Best," he said, pointing to the shorter brunette, "she's the host. The shorter blonde with them is an assistant." He shrugged and sipped his beer. "I don't know them. I just happened to be there when the assistant was talking to the organizer. They're here for the show. Want to do a segment on bachelor auctions, I guess."

"So they aren't here to bid on bachelors," Devon said, his hopes sinking by the minute.

"Got no idea."

"Well, there's one way to find out," Devon said. He moved toward the woman, but Todd stopped him.

"Whoa, where are you going? Evanne wants us up on stage. We're next."

"Already? They've barely started this thing."

"Sorry, bro. If you haven't talked yourself up to the women yet, you're out of time. You should have jumped on the chance when you had it."

Brilliant. Up for auction and the only woman openly interested was the last woman he cared to go on a date with. He thought of Abigail and the prospect of her winning, and for once he had to agree with his brother—that moving more quickly might have helped his situation.

Now, he'd have to move to the stage and leave the outcome to Fate.

Picking up his drink for one final sip, he hoped the stars would be on his side.

"HERE'S TONIGHT'S FEATURE, ladies. Two wealthy, eligible brothers engaged in a friendly wager to benefit Children's Charities."

Nicole listened while the announcer introduced the crowd to her sexy stranger and the reason the two men were up there together.

Devon Bradshaw, co-chair of Bradshaw Investment Group, and his brother Todd, battling against each other to see who would go for the most money. She took the sheets from Peggy and found their names on the list along with their contact information. No matter how things turned out tonight, she had a perfect excuse to call him up and request a meeting, and circling his name, she smiled at the thought that sometimes her job came in very handy, indeed.

"Here we go, are you ready?" Penny asked, her voice nearly breathless with excitement.

"You know, I can always track him down after the auction. That's what we're here for, right?"

Penny looked at her as if she'd lost her mind. "And interview him about his date with another woman?"

When phrased that way, Nicole didn't like how it sounded, and the sour feeling sucked the last of her doubt away.

Rolling up the pages, she tucked the pen and note pad in her purse. "Only if I lose the auction," she said. "And I won't."

There. She said it. Decision made and final. She was going to win herself a date with a torturously gorgeous man and start having fun for a change. Eve said the station would probably cover her bid, and besides, Nicole couldn't remember the last time she let loose and had a good time. Tonight would be it. The night of rebirth. The night Nicole Reavis took a step forward instead of wallowing in her past.

For over a year, she'd been wrapped up in her problems and the turmoil that had followed. Ever since her mother had come down with cancer, things hadn't been the same. Her parents had been forced to tell her the truth about who she was—or wasn't, more accurately. The news that she'd been adopted had been a shock, had sent her three thousand miles east, away from friends and family and everything she'd known in search of the answers to questions that had come to haunt her.

Between making new friends, settling into a new job, moving to a slice of the country where she still felt like a foreigner, and then this lottery win, she hadn't taken a moment to relax, let her hair down and enjoy.

A distraction might be just what she needed.

And the look from the man on stage promised all kinds of welcome distraction.

"Well, Devon surely looks like he wants you to win," Penny said. "He hasn't taken his eyes off you since he walked up there."

Nicole licked her lips. No, he hadn't. And the more he studied her with those blue eyes whispering unspoken words of promise, the more intent she was to go home the winner.

"Devon, please tell us what you have planned," the announcer said.

He casually turned to the woman on stage and took the microphone, and when he spoke, his voice sent tingles up Nicole's spine. He had a low, whiskey drawl that made every word sound like a private secret shared between lovers, the kind of voice that could spread velvet over your skin just by whispering sweet sensations.

She imagined that voice in the dark, his lips close to her ear, so close his warm breath tickled the hair at the base of her neck.

"We'll hop in my vintage 1959 Cadillac convertible and head north to the new Santiago Resort and Spa in the beautiful Atlanta foothills," he said. "My date will have a choice of how she'd like to spend the day. If she's the outdoorsy type, they offer golf and tennis, or if it's relaxation she's after, there's the full day spa or cruising on the lake."

"Ooh, that sounds divine," the announcer said. "And that's a brand-new resort, ladies. I haven't been but I've heard it's beautiful."

"We'll finish the day off with dinner at the restaurant which sits right on the water's edge," he said. Then he turned and set his gaze directly on Nicole. "And with the right woman," he added raising a brow, "who knows where the night could end."

A million-dollar smile polished off his presentation leaving Nicole weak in the knees and ready to mortgage off the condo if she had to. With no effort, her imagination picked up where his description left off, turning the afternoon date into an adventure of sun, fun and sex.

She'd visited the Santiago Resort for a recent episode where they'd given away a romantic weekend for two. She'd toured the facilities and had no trouble imagining herself in one of those suites, buried under the fluffy down comforter with Devon Bradshaw in the flesh.

The thought swelled her insides and heated her blood, the way it apparently had with the rest of the women in the room. A round of hoots and whistles erupted, and though a number of women voiced their desire for that package, Devon never pulled his gaze from Nicole.

As if to signal her intentions, she smiled and faintly nodded, and the sexy expression on Devon's face brightened to a grin.

"He's mine," Nicole said, twisting the pages in her hand, and when the announcer presented the opening bid, she raised her hand without hesitation.

And so did two dozen other women, but the numbers didn't faze her. She was about to be a millionaire, and even though she didn't have her money yet, staring into those beautiful blues with a weekend of sex on her mind, the sky was her only limit.

The price flew up from a few hundred dollars to over a thousand, and when it hit fifteen hundred, it was only Nicole and two other women.

"I don't know if the station will go this high," Eve said.

"I'll pay for it myself."

Fifteen-fifty and Nicole raised her hand taking the bid to sixteen hundred.

"Oh, my God," Penny beamed. "He just passed the high water mark for the evening."

A tall, too-thin woman, who looked a lot like the animated version of Cruella Deville, seemed as intent to win Devon as Nicole was. It was the same woman she'd seen him talking to earlier, and though that fact gave her pause, Devon's heated stare swept away any doubts. Everything about his expression said he wanted Nicole to win, the smile of promise in his eyes, the sexy quirk of his mouth, right down to the way he rubbed his thumb against his fingers as he held his hand at his side.

It was his only hint of nerves, and Nicole couldn't help but zero in on it. The higher the bid, the faster he rubbed, the faster he rubbed, the more intensely his eyes fixed on her. It was as if he was begging her to keep going, and she smiled, thinking he didn't have to worry.

Nothing would make her stop.

Seventeen, then eighteen hundred, and the third woman finally backed out. Now it was just Nicole and Cruella, who really needed a solid meal more than she needed the date.

Like two opponents in a game of table tennis, the bids bounced back and forth between the two.

Eighteen-fifty, nineteen hundred, nineteen-fifty. Every time Nicole took the bid the other woman took it back and the higher they went, the more annoyed she became.

Who was this nightmare?

Nicole nearly yelled out to tell the woman to give up, now understanding the fierce annoyance that could throw a civilized woman into a cat-fighting frenzy. She felt like storming over and giving her a push.

Not that it would take much.

"That other woman really wants him," Penny whispered.

"I'm taking her out," Nicole replied, not at all feeling like it was the joke she'd intended. The more persistent Cruella was the more aggravated Nicole became. The woman was relentless, like a dog with its teeth clenched tightly on a sock. No matter how many times Nicole raised her hand, she just smiled and raised hers. It was becoming a ridiculous test of wills and checkbooks, and if Devon hadn't continued to encourage her with the pleading look in his eyes, she might have backed out by now.

The price was now topping twenty-five hundred, nearing its way to three thousand, and though she could care less about the money, something about the situation stopped her in her tracks.

The contest between two brothers. The brunette talking casually with Devon before the auction. Her unfailing insistence on keeping up with the bidding and Devon's heated encouragement for Nicole to keep going, to keep raising the price.

Was she being played?

"Nicole," Eve warned. "This is getting pricey. You can't count on the lottery, hon. We might not get our money thanks to Liza's lawsuit against us."

Raising her hand, Nicole took over the bid once more, but this time less intently. She didn't care about the money, but the sudden flash that something here might be foul.

It was all too perfect, her attraction to this stranger, more hot and fiery than anything she'd felt before, all brought on by this undersea Eden set up to breed passion in everyone who entered. There was romance in the air, from the oysters on the half shell to the champagne to the plates of chocolate hearts on the tables.

And to find this instant connection with someone who gave her every signal he felt the very same way? How likely was that to happen? How much of this was simply the act of being swept up into the evening?

In a serious wave of doubt, her mind began spinning backward, rewinding to the first glance, her first impression, trying to recall what started all this and how she got caught up into it. Was this man sending her genuine signals or was he just trying to win the bet against his brother?

"Going once," she heard.

Penny jabbed her in the ribs. "What are you doing? Don't stop now."

With a quick jerk, she raised her hand and took the bid again, now unsure exactly how high it was. Then she tried to shake the clouds from her thoughts.

This was silly, these doubts. If the man was trying to set up the bidding, he would have arranged it ahead of time, maybe with women he already knew. Not once had he approached her. In fact, he hadn't approached any of the women here tonight. While all the other men were making contacts and getting to know the prospective buyers, he'd stood at the bar casually watching the room.

No, she thought. This was real. There was real heat here. Real attraction and she really wanted this date.

"What are you doing?" Penny asked. "You almost lost it."

"She's regaining her senses," Eve said. "Nicky, don't get carried away. Like you said before, you have the man's phone number. You can always call him after the auction."

"No," said Nicole. "I want this."

Up flew her hand to take over the bid again, the brunette still going on as if she could do this all night. And Devon still held his eyes on Nicole—that intense stare focused directly on her, the smile telling her she won't be sorry, and that brush of his thumb caressing back and forth, prompting her to keep bidding.

To keep driving the price up so he can win the bet.

Damn, that voice of doubt. It was the same voice that had been paralyzing her for too many months now.

This was all about her parents and the situation that had stripped away her trust in everything pure and honest. And who could blame her? When the two people she should have believed in most handed her the greatest betrayal, how was she expected to have faith in a stranger in a bar? Maybe a year ago, she would have played into this without thinking twice. She would have taken everything at surface value, never considering that Devon and Cruella were conspiring to win this wager from his brother.

But when her parents were forced to admit they'd lied to her about her birth, her basic trust in human beings was destroyed.

It wasn't even finding out that she was adopted that hurt the most. Millions of children are adopted and grow up with a solid sense of self. It was that her parents had never intended to tell her. That she'd always been led to believe that she was their natural child, that their heritage was her heritage, their culture her culture.

That she was a Reavis, and Reavis's were doers and go-getters and survivors. It was in her blood, who she was.

And only when her mother became ill and the

truth leaked out were her parents forced to confess the family secret.

Everything she had, everything she was had been a lie. And Nicole hadn't been the same person since learning the truth.

"What are you doing?" Penny pleaded. "You're going to lose!"

"Going once," the announcer said.

"She's wising up. This is too much money," Eve said.

And in the midst of it all, Nicole's mind went blank with confusion, halting her from taking action or knowing which way to turn. The same way it had every time she tried to make a move with her life or to find the answers she'd been seeking.

Perpetual limbo. Handed down by Don and Betty Reavis to their grown daughter.

"Going twice," the announcer said.

"Come on," Penny urged. "You're going to be a millionaire. Who cares about the price? Get the guy, already!"

"I don't…"

Nicole didn't know what to do. Fixing her eyes on Devon's she saw a mist of disappointment. A gentleman, he tried to hide it for the audience, but she could see the falseness in his smile. It wasn't the same smile of expectation he had a moment ago, and she wondered if it had turned because she wouldn't end up as his date or because the price hadn't gone as high as he'd hoped.

Closing her eyes, she fumed. This was silly. Ten seconds ago, she was having a great time, anticipating a romantic date with the first man to warm up her insides in as long as she could remember. The chemistry was real. So why was she standing here doubting it all?

What happened to the old Nicole who went for what she wanted, reached out and grabbed the brass ring without worrying whether or not it was just worthless plated steel?

What happened to the doer, the go-getter, the woman who made things happen?

"Sold for three-thousand-five-hundred dollars!" the announcer said.

Sold to another woman, Nicole conceded, pulling her gaze away from Devon and turning from the stage.

"I can't believe you let him go!" Penny cried.

She looked to Eve and Penny. Only Eve knew the truth about why she'd come to Atlanta, but even so, she still couldn't explain why she could be confident one moment then a pile of hesitation the next.

Heck, even she didn't get it. So instead, she lied.

Sticking up her chin, she pasted on a smile. "Eve was right. The price got too high."

"But—" Penny started.

Nicole held up the crinkled pages in her hand. "I've got his phone number right here, remember? Let the woman have her date. I'll catch him on the rebound."

3

NICOLE PULLED THE PEN and notepad from her purse and recorded Devon's auction result as she had the others. On stage, his brother, Todd, was selling the crowd on his date, and when the bidding kicked off, a flurry of hands went up promising that the wager between siblings could be a very tight race.

Next to him, Devon stood by idly watching the proceedings. A few times he'd glanced over, winked or smiled in a no-hard-feelings kind of way, but aside from that he'd kept his attention on the show. He'd moved on, his focus back to his brother and the auction and no doubt the woman who'd be enjoying his fantasy date.

And the longer Nicole stood there the more foolish she felt for backing out the way she had. She'd been having a good time doing something wild and spontaneous. She'd seen something she wanted and had decided to go for it.

For that moment, she'd been her old self again, and it felt good. She shouldn't be standing here noting the fact that another woman would go home with her prize. She should be standing by the stage waiting for Mr. Delicious to come down and take her hand.

"There's three thousand, do I have three thousand one hundred?" the auctioneer announced.

Two women held up hands leaving Nicole all but certain Todd would win. The auction hadn't even slowed and already the price had neared the thirty-five hundred Devon went for.

"I'm sorry, but no date is worth that kind of money," Eve said.

"Tell me about it," Nicole murmured then vowed to believe it.

Eve was right. She shouldn't be making such a big deal out of this. It was just a stupid date that would have cost her more money than she had at the moment. Instead of complaining she should be pleased she'd come to her senses when she had.

"I'll throw in a dozen roses," Todd said when the bid hit Devon's, and when one woman raised her hand and made Todd the winner, the crowd erupted. With the bidding still going, he raised his arms in victory and did a happy dance on stage, leaving Devon rolling his eyes on the sidelines. A few more bids widened the margin before Todd's date finally sold for three thousand eight hundred, relieving the two brothers from their presence on stage.

And of course, waiting by the stairs to be the first to claim her trophy was Ms. Cruella Skin-And-Bones. Nicole turned her attention to her notes, not interested in standing witness to the grand induction.

"Well, that was exciting," Nicole said, trying to shake off her disappointment and move on with the evening. "They've raised over twelve thousand dollars so far and they're only halfway through their list of bachelors."

"I wonder if they've got any more dueling brothers," Penny said. "That was amazing. If I wasn't so broke, I would have gone after Todd. He's almost as adorable as his brother."

"Hopefully, we'll get a lot of responses on the flyers the organizers are passing out to the winning bidders," Nicole said, again trying to yank the discussion off Devon and onto something more pleasant.

"We should. Most people love the idea of getting on TV," Eve said. "It wouldn't surprise me to show up at the station Monday with a dozen voice mail messages."

"I wonder how many people end up seriously involved after these dates. You know? Like, how many marriages come out of bachelor auctions," Penny speculated.

The image of Devon and Cruella at the altar flashed in Nicole's mind, making her seriously wish she'd left Penny at home tonight.

"Probably not many," Penny added. "But I'll bet the bulk of them end up at least doing it. I mean, you have to consider the odds and—"

"Can we stop talking about this, please?" Nicole took a breath, hoping to calm her aggravation when a familiar voice sounded behind them.

"I'm disappointed in you, Nicole. I thought I had my lead story for tomorrow's broadcast."

It was Stella Graves, *The Grave Digger,* as the crew at CATL-TV called her. Stella was the entertainment reporter for their rival television station, WTVU. Nicole should have known she'd be sniffing around at this auction tonight. The woman had managed to make a local celebrity of herself by nosing about town speculating on the comings and goings of prominent people in the city. Until recently, only Eve had been notable enough to get an occasional mention in Stella's nightly gossip segments, and even then it was rare, most likely because WTVU wasn't keen on giving publicity to its competitors.

But the lottery changed all that. If the win itself hadn't been big enough news, the scandal created by Liza's return made them all ripe pickings for anyone looking for a story. And Stella Graves had been right at the front of the pack.

"Granted," Stella continued, "the friendly wager between the Bradshaw brothers might be a fun mention, but I'd been rooting for you to win. Atlanta would love to know their favorite lottery winners were spending their fortunes buying bachelors."

Forcing a stiff smile, Nicole replied, "Sorry I couldn't help you, Stella."

The woman turned back to the stage and sighed from under the brim of her black felt hat. Part of

Stella's image was to look as though she'd just
flown out from Hollywood, though Nicole had been
there enough times to know few Hollywood locals
actually dressed like her. In California, the wide-
brimmed hats and rhinestones were more commonly
found on drag queens and stage performers, though
in all irony, Stella somehow made it work, coming
across as more eccentric than foolish.

And be damned if Atlanta didn't love her, which
made the subjects of her nightly segments all that
more annoyed.

Stella spoke through a huff and glanced toward
Devon and Cruella. "That Abbey Westlaw certainly
isn't news. If I devoted my segments to all the men
she dates, I wouldn't have time to report on anything else." She raised a brow and added, "Looks
like your Devon will be the next notch on her
bedpost, if he's not there already. They do look as
though they already know each other, wouldn't you
say?"

Nicole gritted her teeth and eyed Eve who shot
a look that said let it go. They'd all dealt with Stella
enough to know this was how she incited news for
her segments. Push a few buttons and people were
likely to say all kinds of things they'd find repeated
on the next day's taping.

"So," Stella added. "Have you got your eye on a
consolation prize?" She motioned toward a tall
blonde near the stage. "That hunk over there looks
appetizing. They say he owns a construction com-

pany. He's not quite as handsome as Devon Bradshaw, but he could certainly build you your dream house."

"Actually," Nicole replied. "I'm done bidding." She shoved the notepad at Penny. "Keep track of the auction for me. I'm getting a drink."

She didn't ask Eve to join her, needing instead to get away from everyone and clear the garbage from her mind. This whole situation was ridiculous at best. It was bad enough moping over losing a date with Devon. Allowing a local gossipmonger to make her feel even worse tipped the scale to absurd.

Since when had men become such a prized commodity anyway? They came a dime a dozen and she could get any one she wanted without having to fork out thousands of dollars. So she'd come across a guy she found attractive. Big whoop. It wasn't the first time, it wouldn't be the last.

And as soon as she convinced herself of all that, she'd be fine.

She found one seat available at the bar, slid into it and calmed herself while the bartender finished with his other orders and came down toward her end.

He slid a cocktail napkin in front of her. "What can I get you?"

"I'll have a glass of chardonnay."

Nodding, the man turned, poured her glass and set it on the napkin. "That's eight-fifty."

She reached into her purse, but before she could

pull out her wallet, a familiar low drawl sounded over her shoulder.

"It's on me."

One masculine hand slid a twenty across the bar, and when she followed it up to the man attached, she found herself staring squarely at two stunning blue eyes.

Her mouth opened, but nothing came out. If Devon Bradshaw had been handsome from across the room, he was doubly attractive just inches from her nose. His broad chest was wider than she'd noted before, the dimple in his cheek deeper, and the blue of his eyes so vivid they were nearly violet. He leaned against the bar, the motion stretching the dress shirt under his opened suit jacket and relieving any doubt that what lay underneath was one solid mass of chiseled joy.

She fought a gut instinct to reach out and touch him, opting instead to take a breath, and what she got was a lungful of fresh, woodsy aftershave that drugged her thoughts of everything but him...naked.

"Thank you" was all she could say, and even that came out slightly hoarse.

His smile broadened. "Considering what you almost paid for a date, this is the least I could do."

Clearing her throat, she took a sip of her wine, then managed to utter, "Almost."

He slid his empty glass across the bar and motioned to the bartender for another. "Well, it's better you didn't win the bid. I'd rather take you on a date free of charge."

She blinked then blinked again. "Take me on a date?"

"If you'll let me."

The way he flashed that smile, that eager boyish grin, she doubted any woman could turn down his request—doubted any of them had.

He held out a hand. "I'm Devon Bradshaw."

Taking it in hers, the warmth of his grasp sent a spray of tingles over her skin, and she now realized for certain that all the silly doubts she'd had about him during the auction amounted to nothing more than her own paranoia. His manner was too genuine, the heat too temperate.

She had, for certain, blown the opportunity to take the date she wanted, the date that should have been *hers*. It was a mistake she wouldn't make a second time.

"Nicole Reavis."

"Nicole," he repeated, letting the word roll over his tongue as if he was trying it on for size. "It's a pleasure."

"Um," she started, getting back to the subject at hand. "I thought you already had a date." She scanned the room for Cruella. The woman had just forked out three grand for the man. Wasn't it somewhat rude for him to be here buying her drinks?

Devon jerked his thumb toward the auction. "She's moved on to her next acquisition."

Nicole gaped. "She's bidding on someone else?"

He smiled and shook his head. "Abbey's an

old…friend, a real estate broker with some strange ideas on how to drum up new business."

Nicole searched the crowd and sure enough, Cru—er, Abbey, was back at the auction bidding on the next guy.

"So she's—"

"Nothing more than a friend," Devon said. "What I'd really like to do is get out of this fish tank and spend my evening with the woman I *am* interested in." Taking her hand, he brushed his thumb over the back of her fingers. "Have dinner with me tonight."

She glanced at the crowd and at Eve and Penny, who'd somehow managed to ditch Stella Graves. She really shouldn't leave them here to deal with work alone. Although, on the other hand, they'd already accomplished what they'd come for and that was to meet with the organizers and get a sense of the auction. Even taking notes on the bidding results had been overkill since she probably could obtain the information from the organizers. They'd been so excited about the additional publicity of being on Eve's show, they were willing to hand over anything they needed.

But still, the three women were here together, and though they'd taken separate cars—

She stopped.

She took a breath then wondered what the hell she was doing. Had she learned nothing tonight?

Closing her eyes briefly, she vowed that for the rest of the evening, there would be no more

doubts, no more suspicions and no more ques-
tioning every turn she made. Her sexy bachelor
was offering her the second chance to let her hair
down and have a good time.

So without giving another second's thought to
what she should or shouldn't do, she turned to
Devon, smiled and said, "Yes. I'd love that."

DEVON SHIFTED IN HIS seat for the third time since
they'd taken a table at Portobano's restaurant a few
blocks from the auction. As if this wonderful
evening needed anything more, his dinner with
Nicole answered the age-old question: It *was*
possible to get a hard-on just watching a woman eat.

Advertisers had been attempting the feat for
years, running with the assumption that sex can sell
anything from cars to sloppy burgers. Up until now,
he hadn't bought it. But for an hour now, Devon's
dick strained every time she slid that fork in her
mouth and licked those luscious pink lips.

And it didn't help that she found the meal delectable. When she'd taken that first bite of her
lobster raviolis, her expression rolled into that of
divine pleasure, a blissful look that he could only
imagine seeing between the sheets, under his
naked body, after he'd sent her over the brink
into ecstasy.

She did the same thing with the green beans, the
bite of steak he offered, his mashed potatoes and
everything else he could convince her to taste. He

needed to back off before she either caught on or he succumbed to his desire to duck under the table and move on to dessert.

"So you've just got the one brother," he said in a valiant attempt to get his mind out of his pants and onto the beautiful woman seated with him.

"Yep, it's just me and Nate," she said. "He's still in San Francisco."

"And what had you packing your bags and moving across the country if all your family's out west?"

"I was looking for a change of pace. Experience the world, kind of thing."

There was a blankness to the statement that made it sound canned, but Devon didn't press. Maybe she'd just been asked the question a lot. It wasn't every day a television producer moved from a big market like San Francisco to a city half its size to take on a show even smaller than that.

As she brought another bite of ravioli to her mouth, he asked, "And how do you like Atlanta so far?" prompting her to stop.

She considered for a moment then said with resolve, "It's good to get away."

"From?"

"My family. That's what I was looking for by coming here. I needed some space and time." She set the fork back down on her plate. "My mother's cancer took a lot out of me, made me see things differently. And when she went into remission, she didn't need me so much anymore."

"That's all very understandable."

"But it's not only that." She stared into space as if she were trying to put together the right words. "It was sort of time for me to get away from it all and find out who I was and what I wanted from life, without the distraction of all the opinions around me."

Devon couldn't help but laugh. "I understand completely." And he did. He wondered if her leaving San Francisco came with the same uproar he would probably get when he announced to his father he wasn't interested in the family business. Regardless, Nicole was here in Atlanta looking to find her own way which was the example he needed to follow.

"Sometimes family ties can feel more like shackles," he said. "I admire your courage to make a break from it all. It's something I plan to do myself when the time is right."

"You don't like running an investment company?"

"How do things like bond trading and corporate acquisitions and capital funding sound to you?"

She smirked and confessed, "A little dull."

"A lot dull. I only suffered through economics in college because I thought life would get more interesting once I was running the show."

"But it hasn't."

"Not by a mile."

Taking a sip of her wine, she pushed her plate away signaling the end of her meal, and Devon breathed a sigh of relief. The woman was sexy to distraction, so seductive the simple act of chewing made him hot under the collar. Not that it was a bad thing. He couldn't remember the last time a woman lit so many nerve endings. Not since those lustful days of puberty, when anything with breasts turned him on, had he been so wired over a woman.

The problem was, he was enjoying getting to know her and discovering the things they had in common. He'd like to keep his focus on the conversation rather than the many ways she could unwittingly arouse him.

"So, what *do* you want to do?" she asked.

"I want to build things. At the end of the day, I'd like to have created something that didn't exist that morning. That's what I don't like about what we do. Bradshaw Investment Group doesn't produce anything tangible. Basically, we help rich people get richer."

"But this country is founded on commerce. You may not be building things yourself, but you're providing avenues for those that do."

"For a fee we find people the backing they need. But we're just the money end of it, and even then, we aren't paying for anything. We're brokering in the middle, neither offering the cash nor creating a product." He set his knife and fork on his plate and pushed it aside. "I guess I'd like to do something that really matters."

"And how do you think your family will react when you break the news?"

He took a sip of his wine and considered the question. Before now, he hadn't really put thought to how his father would react to the idea of him stepping down from the company. Though he'd joked to himself about a backlash, when pressed to really consider, he gathered the man would be more hurt than upset. The business was his pride, his life's work. He'd wanted all his sons to keep going what he'd nourished, and though he'd been realistic enough to know not all the kids would want it, Devon doubted his father would expect him to be the one to opt out.

Devon had always been the easy one, the kid that went along and never made waves. And he supposed in order to please his parents he felt he owed them a shot at taking over the business. But now that he had, he'd confirmed this wasn't the life for him, and though pleasing the folks was one thing, living for them was an entirely different matter.

"I don't know," he said. "How did your parents feel about your move to Atlanta?"

She shrugged. "I think they were as upset with the career change as the move. The show I produced back in San Francisco had a lot more exposure than *Just Between Us*. That and they've only got me and my brother, Nate. I think my parents had wanted a bigger family, but it didn't turn out that way. With just the two of us kids, it's been even harder for them that I moved away."

He sensed an undercurrent of discomfort every time she spoke of her family, as if there was more going on where that was concerned. So he backed off the subject, preferring to leave his first dates on a high note—this one in particular, since he was hoping this would be the first of many.

Backing from the table, he motioned for the check then asked Nicole, "How would you like to go for a drive?"

The fire returned to her eyes. "Do you really own a 1959 Cadillac convertible?"

"Yes, and I happen to have it with me tonight."

"This is Gabe," Devon said after they left the restaurant and made their way to where he'd parked his old Caddy. He motioned to the car, a monstrous red Cadillac with white interior and a white canvas roof. "Gabe, meet Nicole."

"You call your car Gabe?"

"Every old car needs a name. Gabe just seemed to fit."

She chuckled. "Please don't tell me you're one of those people who names their home, too. That's so pompous."

"No, just the car...and a stuffed alligator named Crikey, but I don't usually talk about that on first dates."

He opened the passenger side door and she slid in, one long, silky leg after the other, and he had to remind himself he'd vowed to remain a gentleman tonight. Every moment he spent with Nicole furthered his feeling that she was the one, the woman he'd been waiting for to come along and turn his head. When it came to the right woman, Devon never had a specific list of attributes he was looking for, but always felt he'd know her when he found her.

And tonight confirmed that notion.

He wanted to see a lot more of this woman, which meant she wouldn't be his one-night-stand. He'd made enough mistakes in his past to learn how to approach that one lover he wanted to keep, and now that he'd found her, he intended to learn from them.

His every move tonight would be honorable, right down to leaving the evening with nothing more than a goodnight kiss.

Even though it would probably kill him.

Slamming the door, he rounded Gabe and slipped into the driver's seat, then turned the ignition and started them on their way.

Nicole looked behind them. "This thing's a boat. How do you avoid hitting things?"

"I don't," he teased. "The beautiful thing about cars like these is you can run them into a train and step away without a scratch."

She smiled. "I'll take your word for that one."

"Seriously, I don't drive it often. It sucks up gas and you can't park it anywhere. I only pull it out of the garage once a week to keep the juices flowing. It's a real kick on a day when the temperature's just right. I put the top down and take it for a spin."

He pulled onto the street and drove her out of town, making his way toward one of his favorite vista points overlooking the city. He loved how readily they could talk, the easy comfort of her company and that west coast manner she had of speaking her mind without thought to propriety. It was refreshing, stepping away from the typical guessing games and double-speak he'd had to deal with on other dates.

She pointed to the red tomahawk hanging from his rear view mirror. "You can't be a Braves fan."

"Till the day I die."

She sighed and shook her head. "And here I thought you had such promise."

"Oh, come on. What's wrong with the Braves?"

She quirked her brow and crinkled her nose in a way that made him want to kiss it. "How much time do you have?"

"So I suppose you wouldn't be interested in going to a game with me one of these days."

"And suffer through that stupid tomahawk chop and that incessant chanting? There's not enough aspirin on the planet to get me through that."

He deadpanned, "You're a Giants fan."

She smiled. "Till the day I die."

"Do you think we can get past this?"

"No, I'm afraid I'm just going to have to use you then toss you aside with the other Major League misfits."

Her wink said she was only kidding, but he still

found himself picking up speed, interested in finding out more about how she might intend to use him.

She glanced into the backseat. "Speaking of which, there's sure a lot of room in here. I'll bet a couple could do all kinds of things in the backseat of this puppy."

The comment nearly prompted him to pull over right there. He could think of a half dozen things he'd like to do with Nicole in the backseat of his Caddy, and her expression said she'd already considered several of them. If he'd intended to remain a gentleman tonight, this drive might have been a bad idea.

"Like?" he asked, not entirely sure he'd be able to handle her answer.

"Come on," she teased. "A guy doesn't have a car like this just for the bad gas mileage. These bench seats are roughly the size of a small bed. And you know," she added, tugging at the belt at her waist, "they don't make seat belts like they used to." She flicked a brow. "I imagine these could hold a guy pretty firmly in place while a woman has her way with him."

Was she talking bondage? The arid wasteland that had become his mouth said she was.

"I actually hadn't considered that one," he said, his voice hindered by a slight wheeze.

Unbuckling her seat belt, she slid over the long bench seat and placed an arm around his shoulder, resting her other hand on his thigh. Every muscle in his body twitched with electricity, and when he turned onto the access road to the vista point, he had to work hard to keep himself from barreling down the road.

"And here I thought you were a man with a vivid imagination," she said, her lips close to his ear.

"You know, it's dangerous to ride without a seat belt," he said, his voice getting tighter by the minute.

"Then you should probably pull over pretty soon."

Sliding her hand farther up his thigh, she stopped right before the junction of his legs and an erection quickly moved in to take up the space.

His hands sweaty and his neck tight with anticipation, he made the final turn and brought the car to a stop at the turnabout where a splattering of cars had parked to enjoy the view.

This spot offered a beautiful view of the valley and the night was exceptionally clear, but for all it mattered, they could have been parked behind a warehouse by the railroad tracks. The moment he turned off the ignition, Nicole snaked her hand up the nape of his neck and moved her body closer, the flowery scent of her perfume filling his senses, her tender touch aching his loins.

"Was this fast enough?" he asked, knowing the question would pull him far off the track of remaining a gentleman this evening. Nicole had all but nixed that idea the moment she placed her hand on his thigh, and though he'd still like to end the evening with his honor intact, that idea was becoming more doubtful by the moment.

She repositioned herself, moving up onto her knees, then straddling his lap, placing her body between him and the steering wheel then lacing her hands around his neck.

"Yeah," she said, her voice breathy with sex and her lips a mere inch from his. She brushed the tip of her nose against his and teased him with a look filled with intent.

He raised his hands to her waist and squeezed, and her resulting shiver raised his temperature another notch.

The woman was insanely gorgeous and delightfully bold. In the darkness of the night, her sun-kissed features took on an erotic shade of gold, and the shadows shrouded her in a new kind of mystery.

She nudged her nose against his ear and sucked in a breath when he slid his hands up her waist and caressed his thumbs against her breasts.

"You can touch them, you know," she whispered, then guided one hand down to her thigh. "Or are you a leg man?"

His dick hardened to steel while his will dissolved into space, and unable to answer the question, he simply nudged his lips to hers and crushed them with a kiss.

Her muscles tensed with heat then softened as if her whole body sucked in a breath then relaxed in his embrace, and he responded by groaning out a statement of unadulterated pleasure. The woman tasted of cream and felt like spun satin, and as he ran his hands over her, her moans of need urged him on.

She was going to kill him. Hot, ripe and ready, she claimed him with every brush of her tongue against his. She cupped his chin with her hands, driving the kiss deeper, sucking his gentlemanly intentions and chivalrous honor right out of him. Her body pulsed against his, her legs tightened at his waist, and when he slid his fingers up to the junction at her thighs, the liquid heat had him nearly bursting in his pants.

"Oh, God," he groaned, but the words drowned in her mouth, lost in the passion between them. He slipped his thumbs up under her panties and brushed them against her folds, and when she sucked in a sharp breath, he knew he was a goner.

Condoms. There were condoms in the glove compartment. He was almost certain.

Sliding her hands down between them, she yanked against the seat belt and snapped open the lock, never once moving her lips from his. His mouth had become her mouth, his breath her breath, and if she was doing what he thought she was doing, the rest of their bodies were about to join as well.

He could feel her pulse in his hands, light moisture over her skin, and when she finally pulled away, he saw a fiery look in eyes filled with need.

"Tell me you've got condoms," she said, the tone closer to a beg than a question.

He nodded, the affirmation bringing a smile of intention to her face. She unfastened his slacks and pulled the waistband down to his thighs, his hands never leaving the soft mounds of her ass. With the clothing pushed aside, his cock sprung between them, firm, hard and ready for whatever she had in mind.

"Ooh," she groaned in a tone that spoke of pleasant surprise.

"You like what you see?"

"Oh, yeah," she said, then pressed her lips close to his ear and added, "I'm just trying to decide whether I want to ride it or taste it."

His cock jerked, his heart pounding heavy as more blood rushed to his loins. Did she have any clue what she was doing to him?

Sliding her hand between them, she palmed his erection and whispered in his ear. "Mmm, so many choices."

Given the way she worked him, Devon feared her choices were about to blow. Gently, she slid her fingers over his shaft, caressing the soft tip with her thumb then gliding her hand down lower and tickling his balls. He swallowed, trying to hold on to his composure by concentrating on the heat between her thighs. Brushing his thumbs against her folds, the wet need greeted him, prodding him to go farther, and he responded by slipping a thumb inside.

She gasped and answered, "Yes," as he began pumping his thumb in and out, matching the rhythm of her hand around his shaft. She began rocking against him, the two of them falling into a motion that would soon bring them to completion if one of them wasn't careful. And Devon feared it would be him. She'd soaked his hand with her sex, the sweet scent permeating the space around them and driving him further toward the edge while her fingers touched just lightly enough to keep him aching for more.

The woman was good. Real good. Holding him right where she wanted him, on that searing edge where his climax threatened yet remained unfulfilled.

For the moment.

A bead of moisture leaked from his tip and she dabbed it then licked it off her finger, the sexy look in her eyes nearly sealing the deal right there.

"You're driving me crazy," he groaned, thrusting his thumb deeper inside while he braced her hip with his other hand. Her eyes grew heavy, as if her own orgasm was near, and Devon decided if he didn't get inside her right now, this evening would end on a humiliating note.

"I think it's time for a condom," he urged, motioning toward the glove compartment, which now seemed like a trillion miles away. He couldn't come close to reaching, and when she backed off to get them herself, her rear end hit the horn, setting off a blare so loud it could have wakened the dead.

Outside he heard the friendly beeping of neighboring cars and distant laughter, reminding him that there were other people around. And if that weren't bad enough, a rap on the window halted them both in their tracks.

He looked at Nicole, her cheeks flushed and her lips chafed with sex. She was still straddling him but now checking her dress to assure nothing was exposed, and he followed suit by pulling his pants back up his waist and quickly, but carefully, zipping his fly.

When they seemed to be in order, he reached out and rolled down the steamy window to come face to face with the flashlight of a Georgia State Ranger.

The man raised a brow when he spotted Devon and Nicole, thankfully not taking the time to study them too closely. He'd probably been down this road more times than he could count.

"Aren't you a tad old for this?" the man asked.

Devon opened his mouth with no idea what to say, and before he could, Nicole answered for him.

"Too old for sex?"

He turned his eyes to her, not believing what she'd just said.

"For public indecency," the ranger said rather humorlessly.

Nicole got the hint and slid off Devon's lap.

"I'm sorry, sir," Devon said. "We were enjoying the view and got carried away." Nicole's snicker left him fighting to keep a straight face. He didn't know what the park rangers were like in California, but in the South they demanded respect.

"You and every teenager up here." The man scowled at him then turned the frown to Nicole. "I think you kids should move the party back home."

Kids?

"Yes, sir," he said. "Absolutely." And when he heard the snap of Nicole's seat belt, he knew the party was over.

4

"I CAN'T BELIEVE YOU two got busted by a park ranger!" Eve said. She and their coworker, Jane Kurtz, sat across the conference table at CATL-TV, their eyes wide with disbelief.

Nicole chuckled. "He told us to take the party home."

"So you did, right?" Eve asked.

Nicole's smile faded. "Not exactly. We started back toward town but before we could even talk about what to do next, his brother, Todd, called needing a ride home." She frowned. "I don't know why the guy couldn't call a cab, but the next thing I knew, Devon was dropping me off at my car, kissing my cheek and asking for my phone number. Our evening ended in the parking garage across from the club."

"Oh, wow, that is such a riot."

"So do you think he'll call?" Jane asked.

Nicole shrugged. "I don't know. He probably thinks I'm a sex-starved lunatic, coming on to him like that in the front seat of his car."

Though she had to admit, it had been fun to step

away from her problems and let loose for a change, to forget about the confusion that had zapped her spirit and left her wandering life like a stray dog.

For over a year, she'd been trying to process her adoption and all the issues surrounding it. She didn't want to be angry with her parents, but no matter which way she turned it over in her mind, she couldn't understand why they did what they did, why it had been so important to them that she believed she was theirs. For her entire life, they'd implanted an identity, and now that identity had been snatched out from under her as if the person she was never existed.

She wasn't a Reavis. Their heritage wasn't her heritage, their culture not her culture, their blood not her blood. Instead, all those things were here in Atlanta, the home of her birth parents. Or at least it was their home twenty-nine years ago when she was born.

Nicole had shown up in town nine months earlier following the urge to find out where she really had come from. If she wasn't a Reavis, who was she?

Admittedly, she hadn't had much of a plan. She figured she'd settle into her job, get to know the area then try to find out as much about her birth family as possible. At the onset, she'd only expected to spend maybe a year in the area researching her family relations. But so far, she hadn't even uncovered a family name. Her parents had only given her a birth date and the name of the center that held her adoption papers. She'd obtained a copy with everything pertinent blacked out. Everything else had been sealed, and so far Nicole hadn't had the time or the energy to start the long process of decoding the rest.

She'd been dragging her feet, telling herself it was the unexpected pressures of the job. But a side of her realized it wasn't even that.

Maybe a side of her didn't want to know.

She'd come here on a mission, her intentions clear, her goals in place. And then like a light switch, it all shut off. Doubt and confusion set in. She'd found herself feeling woefully out of place. Atlanta, Georgia, wasn't California by any means, and instead of moving into town feeling as though she'd come home, she felt like an uninvited guest, an intruder trying to insinuate herself into a place where she didn't belong.

And if she wasn't a Reavis, and she didn't belong here, then who was she and where *did* she belong?

"I've yet to meet a man turned off by a sex-starved woman," Jane said.

"And you should know," Eve said. "It was that wild weekend in Vegas where you got together with Perry, after all."

Jane grinned in that starry-eyed way new lovers always do. Between all of them, Jane had been the most conservative of the bunch, the one who kept her feet firmly set on the floor. Thus, it had come as a surprise to everyone when she'd packed up and taken off to Las Vegas, only to come back in love with her neighbor, Perry Brewer. The two had been an item ever since and if Nicole were a gambler, she'd bank on the fact that marriage was somewhere in their future.

She smiled. "Well, I hope Devon calls. I'd like to finish what we started."

The conference room door opened and in walked Zach Haas and Cole Crawford, the other two CATL members who had won the lottery with the three women. With Liza Skinner coming out of the woodwork and launching a lawsuit, the group had arranged to meet first thing to agree on next moves.

Nicole didn't have much of an opinion when it came to the matter. Having come in after Liza left Atlanta; she didn't know the woman or the history she'd had with the other members of the crew. From the moment the mess started, Nicole had decided she would opt with the majority, going along with whatever everyone else decided.

Unfortunately, it looked like the other four were split, the two women wanting to fight Liza's claims, the men wanting to resolve the matter fast so they could all walk away with their money.

Cole took a seat while Zach closed the door behind them then joined the group at the table.

"All right," Cole said. "We've all been talking amongst ourselves lately, now it's time for some group action."

Eve snorted. "Oh, there's a few things I'd like the group to do with Liza."

Jane placed a hand on Eve's and shot her a look of consolation. From what Nicole had learned, Liza Skinner had been best friends with Eve and Jane, the three women founding the show and practically sisters in every way. Until they had a falling out and Liza left without a word. She'd packed up everything and had taken off without so much as a note explaining where she was going or when she'd be back.

The move had left Jane and Eve in a bind as to what to do. Liza had been the chief segment producer on the show, and expecting she might come back, they hadn't rushed to replace her. Amidst their concerns for her well-being, they'd both worked double-time to fill in for her, until the stress got too high and they were forced to hire Nicole.

Nicole had taken Liza's job and had had to jump in with both feet. From that standpoint, she understood Eve's and Jane's feelings. It hadn't been a small effort to get the show back on track, and when Liza returned without the slightest remorse for taking off the way she did, they were all pretty sour. If she'd just communicated with them, she could have saved everyone a lot of grief. Not to mention the fact that once she *did* come back, her only purpose had been the lottery money and getting what she felt was hers.

Her attitude had been a stab in the chest to the two women who'd thought they were friends.

Cole flashed Eve a stern look. "Let's keep the personal stuff out of it."

"But it is personal. At some point, Liza has to learn she can't walk in and walk out as she pleases, strolling into town and taking what she wants, then shoving off again, be damned with the rest of us. Have you forgotten what she put us through?"

"I haven't forgotten," Cole said. "But we've got an issue here that needs to be resolved, and rehashing the past isn't going to move us forward."

As the show's producer, Cole was always the big picture man of the group, the one who rose above the details to get to the bottom line. He was also the one with more at stake than the rest of them, being a single father of twin girls.

Already, the media had taken an interest in their lives, Liza's lawsuit adding fuel to the flames. The group had become a good story, a local saga that many people had become interested in following, and while it was a mere annoyance for the rest of them, Cole had his daughters to consider. Since his wife broke up their marriage and family, he'd been working hard to make their life as normal as possible, and he was understandably worried about how the media attention might be affecting them.

"I think we need to do whatever it takes to resolve this matter quickly," he added.

"Not if it means giving Liza what she wants. I'd gladly forfeit all my lottery winnings before giving her a cent."

"It's not only your winnings, Eve," Zach said. "That's the problem here. It's not just about you, Jane and Liza. There are three other people involved who need to be considered."

He looked to Nicole for agreement and she responded with a faint nod. Like her, Zach was also fairly new to the group, only having taken his job as camera operator several months earlier. Though their newbie status had given them that bond, Nicole was reluctant to side with Zach wholeheartedly. Of all of them, she understood betrayal and the deep hurt Jane and Eve were dealing with, and she didn't want to side against them.

In fact, she didn't want to side against anyone, and while this lottery win had seemed like a godsend in the beginning, this battle it had created between her coworkers only proved to be another problem on her plate.

A side of her did want to suck it up and settle if it meant they could all move on. But unless everyone felt good about the settlement, none of them would be able to walk away and put this behind them.

"I understand that," Eve said. "And that's all the more reason we shouldn't back down and hand Liza whatever she's asking for. I mean, what if six more people come out of the woodwork claiming a stake in the prize?"

"On what basis?" Cole scoffed.

"Who knows? Liza's claim is ridiculous, yet

she's found a lawyer willing to back her. After that, I wouldn't put anything past anyone."

"I have to agree," Jane said. "We need to draw a line in the sand and demonstrate for everyone we aren't going to give our money away to anyone who demands it."

"Our only other option is to take this to court," Cole said.

"So let's take it to court."

"Court cases can take years, way more time than we have. Remember the deadline. If the winnings aren't distributed within eight months of the drawing, the whole pot is forfeited. There's no way a court case will settle before then."

Eve opened the folder containing the demand letter they'd all received from Liza's lawyer. "She wants an equal share and a public apology. Apology for what? If anything, *she's* the one who should be begging our forgiveness." She closed the folder and shook her head. "I'm sorry, but there's no way I can go that far. We don't owe her anything."

"Is that the way you feel?" Cole asked Jane.

Jane sat quietly for a moment and Nicole could see the hurt in her eyes as she turned the situation over in her mind. Obviously, these wounds ran deep.

After a few seconds of silence, Jane looked to the group and nodded. "I'm sorry, but I agree with Eve. All the money in the world isn't enough for me to apologize to Liza for cutting her out of the winnings. We've done nothing wrong, and I'm not going to sell my integrity."

Cole looked to Nicole. "And you?" he asked.

She opened her mouth, but it took a few beats before she could answer. She really didn't like being in this position. There were five of them and she was the swing vote. Problem was, she agreed with both sides, a truth she knew they wouldn't want to hear, but the truth nonetheless.

"Guys, I don't know what to tell you," she finally said. "I understand Jane's and Eve's feelings. Liza has done nothing but jerk them around, and if I were in their shoes, I'd forfeit my money before allowing her to stomp on me again."

Eve met Nicole's gaze and smiled.

"But," Nicole added, her expression to Eve apologetic. "I'm with you and Zach, too. This isn't just about Eve, Jane and Liza. Zach and Cole and I are in this too, and it's not fair to everyone else to risk losing the money because of this rift."

"So majority rules," Zach said. "We split the pot with Liza?"

"That's not what I said," Nicole defended. "And I don't think this should be a situation where majority rules. We all have to agree. This lottery will destroy us all if we can't find a solution that everyone can live with. Plus, legally I don't think we have a choice. No one can force Jane and Eve to give up a portion of their winnings if they're against it." She looked to Cole for confirmation. "Isn't that right?"

Cole motioned to Eve. "You were contacting a lawyer. What did you find?"

Eve straightened in her seat and cleared her throat. "Yes, I contacted Jenna Hamilton, the station's lawyer. I think most of you have met her on one occasion or another. Is that correct?"

The other members nodded, and though Nicole hadn't met Jenna, she'd heard of the woman and that she had a solid reputation around the office.

"She's willing to take our case if we're all in agreement," Eve said. "In fact, I'd told her we're meeting this morning and she's made herself available in case we'd like to call and talk to her."

The five looked to each other for consent, each of them either nodding or shrugging acceptance of the idea before Cole finally said, "I think Jenna's the closest thing to a lawyer we all know and are comfortable with. I certainly don't have a better recommendation. And I do think, given the circumstances, we should seek legal counsel of our own."

"Yeah, we definitely need a lawyer," Zach said.

"Does everyone else agree?" Eve asked.

The others consented, prompting Eve to pull the phone to the center of the conference table and dial Jenna's number. The whole group needed an initial briefing on where they stood, and after sharing their decision with Jenna, Eve jumped right in with the questions.

"So, she doesn't have a leg to stand on, right?"

"I don't think so," Jenna replied. Her voice was

smooth and reassuring, leaving Nicole with the feeling they'd made a good choice.

"But the laws can get murky where that's concerned," Jenna added. "Add in the fact that this is a state lottery and there aren't many cases out there that are exactly like this one. I've only started looking into old cases, but finding precedents isn't going to be cut and dry, and the thing we don't want to do is blaze our own trail. That can get costly and take a lot of time."

"You realize Lot 'O' Bucks has an eight-month time limit to resolve the dispute or we all forfeit," Cole said.

"That helps and hurts us."

"How's that?"

Jenna explained, "Everyone involved is going to want to see this thing resolved, so dragging our feet—on either side of this—won't be an option. From the start, both parties will want to settle and avoid court proceedings."

"Settle as in give her our money?" Eve asked, a bit too anxiously.

"I'm not saying that. I know you're against it, and from what you've told me, she shouldn't have any claim to the winnings. Her contributions had been exhausted long before you bought the winning ticket."

"Even though technically we were still playing one of the numbers she chose?" Jane reminded.

"I don't see how that can be a factor. Without a written contract, those numbers have no meaning.

For all intents and purposes, they could have been randomly selected."

Eve squeezed her eyes shut as if she were reluctant to ask, "What happens if this *does* go to court? What if we can't settle?"

"Well, let's hope it doesn't go that far. My plan is to respond to the demand letter letting Liza and her lawyer know there's no basis for this suit. This could merely be a scare tactic on her part. Her lawyer might be giving this a shot, hoping you all panic and offer her what she wants."

Zach huffed. "If not, this could end up in court and drag out beyond the time limit."

"The local courts are aware of the time limit and I doubt our elected officials will want to get blamed for a group of lottery winners losing their money. People love lottery winners, the whole Cinderella idea of regular folk winning it big. Regardless of whether people end up on your side or Liza's, they'll want someone to get their money, and so will the lottery board. People won't play if they begin doubting they'll get their money. It's bad publicity all around. That's one of the reasons they made the rule. So people get their money fast."

"So even if it does go to court, we still stand a chance at getting this resolved before the deadline."

The group looked at each other across the table, each of their faces displaying a mix of hope and reservation.

"What have you been saying to the media, by the way?" Jenna asked.

"We all agreed not to comment until we spoke with you," Eve said.

"Keep it that way for now. Let's see what we get and then go from there. We might use the newspapers to our advantage, so let's make sure no one says anything we might have to contradict later on."

They all nodded and gave their assurances.

"And what about the general public. Any problems there?"

Zach chuckled, "You mean all the people calling the station claiming to be long lost cousins? You wouldn't believe how big our families have gotten in the last few weeks."

"Anyone you're worried about?" Jenna asked, the tone in her voice expressing concern.

Eve shook her head. "No. Liza's the only one we're worried about right now and you're already handling her."

"Well, let me know if you or the others have any other trouble where that's concerned. In the meantime, you go back to concentrating on your show. I'll draft a response to Liza's demand and let you know what we get from it." Then her tone turned back to that warm, reassuring manner that left Nicole feeling at ease. "Don't worry. We'll get this worked out and you'll all be the millionaires you deserve to be."

"I like the sound of that," Cole said before they expressed their thanks and ended the call.

The mood in the room immediately turned more positive, each of them apparently feeling the same sense of comfort Jenna had provided Nicole. And now knowing they had help with this lawsuit, Nicole could move her focus to other things.

Like wondering if Devon Bradshaw would be calling for another date.

Leaving the conference room and stepping down the hall toward her office, she recalled her conversation with Eve and Jane before the men walked in. She certainly hoped he'd call. Saturday night had proved how badly she needed to break away from things for a while. She hadn't been on a date since her mother became ill, which was long before she'd moved to Atlanta. She hadn't intended to put her sex life on hold, it just sort of ended up that way.

When she arrived in town she'd been greeted by a job long neglected. The segments were backlogged, shows being thrown together sometimes hours before air time. It had taken Nicole months to play catch-up and get the shows back on schedule, and what free time she had outside of work, she'd been spending researching adoption and the rights adopted children had in getting their records unsealed.

She'd discovered there weren't many. Unless the adoptive parents had made the records available at some point during her life—which hers hadn't— she was legally bound to respect their anonymity.

Granted, there were services available to help in tracking them down, but investigators could be costly and success wasn't guaranteed. For a long while, she'd struggled over what to do, until the lottery win. Tracking down her birth family seemed the right thing to do since she'd been handed the resources she needed to continue her search, and when their winnings had been confirmed, that's exactly what she'd done.

And then Liza ripped it all away, leaving her wondering what Fate was trying to tell her now.

The date with Devon had been refreshing, like taking all the uncertainty in her life and shoving it aside. He'd made her feel like a woman again instead of a lost child and overworked professional. He'd given her passion and lust, laughter and excitement.

And she wanted some more.

The one thing she'd learned in the last year was that answers weren't going to come to her overnight. Stepping off the plane in Atlanta hadn't given her a sense that she was home, and winning the lottery hadn't handed her the key to her past. It would all be more complicated than that, and Saturday night had proved that the best way to deal with a complicated situation was to step away from it on occasion and clear the mind.

And there was no better emotional white-out than Devon Bradshaw. The only question now was whether she should call him or wait for him to make a move.

The sight in her office answered the question.

Sitting on her desk was a giant bouquet of long-stemmed red roses.

An excited Penny sat at the desk next to hers. "Are they from Devon?"

Nicole shrugged and searched for a card. She'd never seen roses so plump and fresh with a hue so vividly red, they looked like velvet.

"Wow," she said. "They take up my whole desk."

"The card's on the other side," Penny gushed. "Hurry and open it. I'm dying to see what it says."

Nicole moved around to the other side of her desk, pulled the card from the folder then burst into laughter when she saw what was inside the envelope.

Along with a card was an orange Get-Out-Of-Jail-Free card from the Monopoly game, no doubt a joke about their encounter with the park ranger. The card itself read,

For our next drive in the Caddy.
When can I see you again?
Devon

"So, what does it say?" Penny urged.

"When can I see you again?"

She took her purse from the bottom drawer of her desk and tucked the Monopoly card in her wallet, smiling over the joke. She imagined handing that to the stone-faced park ranger and doubted it would have gone over well. The man didn't strike her as someone with a sense of humor, but she loved

Devon's joke and the fact that it made her smile. She hadn't been doing enough of that lately.

"That is *soooo* romantic! He's serious about you."

"They're flowers."

"Those aren't any flowers. Do you know where they're from? Di Vonge Florist, it's the priciest place in town." Penny pointed to the giant bouquet. "Those are imported, you know." Then she shook her head with certainty. "A guy who's just having fun doesn't send a woman flowers from Di Vonge."

Nicole scoffed, remembering that Penny was a hopeless romantic. It was one date, they'd had some fun, and the man was just being kind. They were ages from making anything more out of it, and for Nicole that time might be never. She wasn't about to get seriously involved with anyone until she figured out who she was and where she belonged in this world. Everyone knew the age-old saying about not loving someone else until you love yourself. In her case, she didn't even know herself.

"Mrs. Nicole Bradshaw. Doesn't that sound perfect?"

"No, it doesn't," Nicole said. "I have no intention of becoming Nicole Bradshaw." And she meant it.

Her identity had just been wiped clean by her parents, she wasn't about to fill the empty space with the label of wife and mother. In fact, that was all the more reason why she had to keep her intentions in check. Her sense of self was in a vulnerable state right now. Her foundation had been shattered. Without a sense of belonging, it would be easy for a woman to want to find that place with a man, to build a family she knew was hers, to solidify her circumstances by placing a stake in the ground with someone else.

But she knew it would be wrong. Without being at peace with who she was, she'd never be able to fully give herself to someone else, which meant ideas of love and marriage were entirely out of the question.

No. Devon Bradshaw was a fun distraction and that's all, and despite Penny's romantic ideals, Nicole was certain he'd agree there was nothing more to it than that.

5

"I FOUND THE WOMAN I'm going to marry."

Devon smiled at the startled expressions of his dad and brother, Bryce. Surely, they were torn between the idea that he must be joking and the fact that he rarely kidded about things like this. When it came to stepping through life, Devon leaned more toward the conservative side, usually stopping to think about making a move before jumping right in. If anything, he dragged his feet more than he should, turning over every angle before forming a conclusion.

But when it came to Nicole, there wasn't much thinking to do. Though he'd never had an exact image of the woman he was looking for, he'd always felt he'd know her when he saw her, and running into Nicole Saturday night validated that long-held notion.

He saw her. He talked to her. They'd had dinner and he'd held her in his arms. He'd tasted her and had nearly taken her fully, and by the time the night was through, he was certain she was *the one*.

That was it. Heart taken. End of subject.

His father was the first to speak. "Well," he said, adjusting in his seat at the end of the conference table that made up half of Devon's downtown Atlanta office. "When I asked you how your weekend went, that wasn't the answer I'd expected."

William Bradshaw was a tall, slender man and Devon had grown into his exact replica. Both he and his sister, Grace, took after their father, inheriting his searing blue eyes and thick dark hair, while Bryce and Todd had ended up shorter and stockier, like their mother's side of the family.

From as far back as Devon could remember, he'd wanted to be like his dad, maybe not in the sense of his career, but in the way he led his life. The man had a wit about him. He'd always known who he was and what he wanted, and rarely did he make a frivolous move or a decision in haste. With the exception of once, as his story goes, and that was the day he'd met their mother.

Dad always said it took the blink of an eye to know Carol Anne Mayberry was the woman of his dreams, and every time Devon heard the story and witnessed the resulting blush on his mother's face, he knew in his heart that's how love would greet him someday.

And Saturday night, it had, in the form of one tall, sun-kissed blonde who'd shot an arrow through his heart with nothing more than a sexy glance.

"How long have you known her?" his father asked.

Bryce snorted. "What time is it?"

"I met her Saturday."

William raised a brow. "And you already know she's the one?"

Devon turned to his father and winked. "In the blink of an eye."

"Yeah, so what does Devon do?" Bryce chimed in. "He takes her up to The Point and gets busted by a park ranger with his hand up her skirt." He threw his head back and laughed. "How's that for class?"

It never ceased to amaze Devon that for a man pushing thirty, Bryce had never stopped acting as though he were twelve years old. Worse was the man's annoying habit of pulling Devon back to adolescence, as noted by his gut desire to point out the fact that unlike his brother, he'd at least *kissed* a girl in the last twelve months.

If Devon were paying attention—and he wasn't—he might have noticed that since Bryce's college girlfriend broke up with him, he hadn't dated a woman since. And if Bryce were the type to accept any brotherly advice—which he wasn't—Devon might tell him that when a man was as innately picky about women as Bryce was, he should probably try to keep the few that came along.

Instead, he rose above it and casually turned to their father. "I have only honorable intentions when it comes to Nicole."

William raised a hand. "You're grown men now. How you handle your love lives is up to you."

"I realize that," Devon said. "But this one's different. It's important to me that she knows I want more than one thing from her." He turned to his brother and conceded, "I'll give you that The Point probably wasn't the best idea. But I have every intention of taking my time with this one and making it clear that she's much more to me than just a romp in the hay."

"Well, she *does* sound special." William turned and crossed his legs. "Why don't you two come over for dinner so we can meet this woman?" He looked to Bryce. "We'll make it a family affair. Your mother's been complaining that she hasn't had all the kids together since Christmas." Glancing back at Devon, he added. "We're flying down to Florida this weekend, but how about the weekend after?"

Bryce turned to Devon. "Don't you have that date with Abbey you need to fit in?"

"She'll have to work around my schedule. Besides, I haven't even heard from her. I was expecting a call right away, but maybe she's having trouble scheduling all her auction wins."

"Let me check with your mother, but hold the date. And tell Todd next time you see him."

The two men shrugged and agreed.

"So what's this about the audit?" William asked.

Bryce let out a long huff and opened the file he'd brought to the meeting. "We've got problems," he said. "Internal problems."

"Has any of this been confirmed?" Devon

asked, wanting to make sure Bryce wasn't sounding alarm bells unnecessarily. Their father had all but retired from the company, still holding his place as Chief Executive Officer, but hoping his sons could handle business mostly without him. And why shouldn't they? There were three of them doing the job their father had done himself for thirty years. In Devon's opinion, that was at least one son too many. With Bryce handling the financial end of things and Todd cutting most of the deals, Devon didn't have a lot to do.

Unofficially, his job was to keep both brothers in line, oversee their affairs and make sure they knew what they were doing. And for their first few years on the job, it had kept him busy. But despite Bryce's social immaturity and Todd's flippant ways, the two men were running the show pretty well without any additional hand-holding.

Which left Devon thoroughly bored.

"Here's what we know at this point," Bryce said. He pulled out a short stack of papers that Devon assumed were the wire transfers they'd discussed. "The auditors have raised questions about these payments. They're made out to a Reginald Clark as a refund for his investment in the Baywood Project. But we can't find record of him ever investing in Baywood."

He pulled out more papers. "We've got a sudden increase in petty cash withdrawals, but we can't locate any documents approving the funds."

Emptying the file of the last few pages, he added, "And there's over seventy-five thousand dollars in vendor payments to a Carlos Mansano, but there's no note of what services he provided, and no documentation that would give us a phone number or any other identifying information."

"And neither Debbie nor Renee in Accounting recall the transactions?"

"Only that they're positive they didn't make them."

Their father sat for a moment, tapping a finger on one of the transfers while he held his other hand to his chin. His eyes moved from one page to the next as he contemplated the situation.

"How much do you trust Debbie and Renee?" Devon finally asked.

After another beat, William said, "How many other employees have access to the system?"

"Too many," Bryce huffed, his tone clearly frustrated.

For two years now, he'd been complaining about the lack of controls in their accounting processes and the fact that their computer systems hadn't been upgraded since the company expanded four years ago. For most of its history, Bradshaw Investment Group had been a profitable, yet small operation. They'd managed the business with less than ten employees, all family as far as their father was concerned.

But with all the boys stepping into the business, they decided to expand the operation beyond the half-dozen investment partnerships they managed. Todd had been acquiring more partnerships, and Jeff Nelson, their father's former senior executive, had expanded their investing to include venture capitalism, taking advantage of the new information technology trade moving into the area. They'd doubled their staff, but to Bryce's dismay, they had yet to restructure their internal controls to account for their increased exposure to fraud.

"If you've got the password to the accounting system, you've got the ledger and a dozen bank accounts at your disposal," Bryce added. "There's at least six of us with legitimate access, but it wouldn't be difficult for anyone else at the firm to get in, and since we don't even have unique sign-on IDs, we can't even pinpoint whose access at the company might have been breached."

William pursed his lips and studied the pages again, his expression concerned but not as grave as Devon would have expected.

"What are you thinking, Dad?" he asked.

Their father gathered the papers together. "Let me look into a few things." Then he looked at his sons. "Unless there's more."

Bryce shook his head. "That's all we've uncovered so far. Everything else with the audit seems to be in order."

William nodded then placed the pages in the folder and tucked it in his briefcase.

"Bryce is right," Devon said. "I think we should

hire a consulting firm to review our processes and tighten things up."

"Go ahead."

When their father looked as though he were packing to leave, Devon asked. "So…exactly what things do you plan to look into?"

"These men who received the payments, we need to chat with them."

"All we have are their names and bank information, and according to both banks, the accounts closed shortly after the deposits were made."

"I've got people who might be able to find them."

"What people?"

William rose from the table. "People" was all he said. "I'll let you know what they find."

He made his way to the door, tossing over his shoulder, "Don't forget about next weekend," before leaving Devon's office.

The two men stared at each other across the table.

"Don't forget next weekend," Bryce repeated, his deadpan expression stating he was as annoyed as Devon that their father planned to handle this without them. Not only was Devon bored with this job, his father had a way of reminding him that the job wasn't fully his and probably never would be. As long as the man was alive, he'd forever retain final authority, just as his own father had before him.

It was another reminder why Devon needed to get out on his own, become his own man and talk to his own *people* when the need arose. He was capable of being more than an unnecessary middle-man between his dad and his brothers, and as soon as this mystery was solved and any potential storm passed, he intended to do exactly that.

Bryce left the office and Devon returned to his desk aggravated until his cell phone rang and he saw the number.

Flipping open the phone, he smiled. "Hey, beautiful."

Nicole's sweet voice sounded in his ear. "The *roses* are beautiful. And expensive, from what I've been told." And with a tease in her tone, she added, "What can I ever do to thank you?"

The obvious innuendo told him their next encounter might go a lot like their last, and he wondered if those admirable intentions would ever see the light of day.

"Go on a date with me," he said, trying to keep to his personal promise. Though a dozen other ideas had come to mind, he had to make it clear in words and actions that he wanted this thing between them to be more than a tryst. Nicole was special, what they had was special, and before they were through, he'd make certain she knew it was a lot more than physical attraction.

"Hmm," she moaned, and his dick hardened. "I was thinking dinner. My place. Tomorrow night." And with a giggle, she added, "I've cleared the area of all park rangers."

"You typically keep a supply of park rangers at your place?"

Her laugh deepened, the sound warming his mood.

"No, but if you care to show up in the uniform, that might be interesting. Word around the jailhouse is I've been a very bad girl."

His dick turned to steel.

"I may need to be punished," she added.

Then his throat turned to stone.

He swallowed hard and tried to speak. "I thought you had a Get-Out-Of-Jail-Free card?"

She lowered her voice. "I don't know that I want to use it. It might be interesting to see how well the warden handles his gun."

He swallowed again. "Are you trying to kill me?"

"Yes."

"What time?"

"Seven o'clock. Don't be late."

DEVON STOOD IN FRONT of Nicole's high-rise apartment building and checked his watch. Six fifty-nine. Was showing up exactly on time a sign of consideration or desperation? He currently felt both. Though he was generally an on-time kind of guy, tonight, showing up for a date at exactly zero hour had more to do with eagerness than punctuality, and for a split second, he considered walking the block for a few minutes to avoid making it that obvious.

Then he pressed his finger to the button and ended the debate.

"Devon?" he heard through the speaker.

"At your service."

"Come on up," Nicole said, then he heard the click of the glass lobby door indicating she'd tripped the lock. He made his way to the elevator and up to the ninth floor, down the richly colored hallway to number 914. In his hand was another bouquet of flowers, this time pink tulips, and when she opened the door, her eyes lit with a bright smile.

"You look beautiful," he said as he stepped through the threshold and closed the door behind him. And she did. The pale blue sundress and white sandals made a simple canvas that showcased her natural beauty. She wore no make-up other than a light gloss on her lips, and her smooth, tanned legs left him aching for a touch.

He handed her the flowers then pressed a light kiss to her cheek, using the gesture to breathe in her fresh soapy scent.

"How about a drink?" she asked, passing through the short hall and into the main living area where the kitchen and sitting room combined in one large open space. "I noticed you'd ordered bourbon the other night." Holding up a bottle of Bookers, she added, "They tell me this is good."

"I'd love one," he said. Surveying the space, he noted it was decorated exactly as he would have expected, minimal yet tasteful. She allowed the contemporary furniture to stand on its own without the excess adornment of lots of decorative pillows and knick-knacks. She used color and texture to accentuate the room. A white shag throw rug over the dark oak floor defined the seating area that consisted of a sleek orange sofa and matching chair. A glass and maple coffee table held only a couple magazines and a dark blue art glass bowl filled with fresh lemons.

An entertainment center remained hidden in the confines of a large maple cabinet, and opposite it was a floor-to-ceiling view of the Atlanta cityscape. The wall to his right consisted entirely of white painted built-ins filled with books, photographs and other mementos, and curious to know more about his new love, he stepped over and began perusing the shelves.

Pointing to a somewhat grotesque ceramic bust, he had to ask the question. "What's this?"

Chuckling, she crossed the room with his drink and a glass of white wine. "Nate made that for me when he was six years old. It's supposed to be me."

He studied the purple blob that wouldn't resemble a human at all if it weren't for an obvious nose and eyes. "I don't see a resemblance."

"Good answer."

He pointed to a photo of her and a man he suspected might be her brother. The two had similar blue eyes and blonde hair, although the resemblance ended there. "Is that your brother?" When she nodded, he added, "Are you two close?"

"Very," she said. "In fact, this is the longest I've gone without seeing him. When I moved to Atlanta he came with me to check out where I planned to live and where I'd be working. The fact that I'm in a high-security building on the ninth floor is all Nate and Dad."

"I get the high security building, but what's with the ninth floor?"

"Too high for someone to break in from the balcony, but low enough for a fire truck ladder. Ladders only go as high as ten stories. Did you know that?"

"No, I didn't."

She rolled her eyes. "Neither did I, but those are the kinds of things my family thinks about when the baby moves away."

He studied the picture again, two cheeks pressed together and bright smiles grinning for the camera, and he wondered if Nate would want to check him out.

"Do you miss Nate?" he asked.

"Yeah, I do. He's an architect and keeps a busy schedule, but he's been hinting about coming to visit lately. The way Nate is, he could show up any minute unannounced. He tends to fly by the seat of his pants sometimes."

"Well," he said, his body warming from the drink and his close proximity to Nicole. "Let's hope he doesn't show up unannounced tonight. We've already been rudely interrupted once."

"Twice if you count both the park ranger and your brother Todd."

Devon winced. "I guess the two were conspiring that night to keep me an honorable man."

The smile on her face turned from playful to seductive. "Well, there's nothing keeping you honorable tonight," she said, licking her bottom lip and turning him from warm to hot with the one simple statement.

She moved closer and ran a finger up the buttons of his cotton shirt, studying each one of them as if she were contemplating how quickly they could come apart.

"In fact," she added, "I may have to confiscate your cell phone for the evening."

Without another thought, he pulled it from his pocket and placed it in her hand, and after flipping it open and shutting it off, she set it on the bookcase. "No more conspiracies," she said.

She placed a hand on his chest and a wash of heat moved through her touch, spilling through his body and hardening him on the spot. He'd come here expecting a nice dinner, casual conversation and a parting kiss on the lips, all the things a chivalrous man does when he wants to show a woman he's interested in more than her body.

And less than five minutes alone with her it all went out the window.

Those lips were too close, those breasts too supple, those legs too silky and that scent too inviting. No more conspiracies? On the contrary, every part of her body had come together to spin him into her web of seduction, and when she pressed her lips to his chin and took a small bite, he held up the white flag and surrendered.

He clamped his hands to her waist and she gasped with delight, and when he brought his mouth to hers, her resulting moan nearly buckled his knees. The fruity taste of her, the tender press of her lips, the firm lines of her waist all worked together to boil him over with need. His cock hardened, his thighs stiffened, and when she brushed her waist against him and moaned again with pleasure, he wondered if they could make it to the bedroom or if they should both just drop to the floor.

Instantly, his mind began warring between physical desire and the impression he wanted to make with Nicole, and in a last-ditch effort to regain control of the evening, he pulled his lips from hers and whispered in her ear.

"What's for dinner?"

"Me."

Bad answer.

Pulling back, he smiled, not at all liking the flush of her cheeks or the dark look of sex in her eyes. He was supposed to be a good boy tonight and that take-me look on her face was making that nearly impossible.

"You're for dessert," he teased, trying to lighten the moment. "What are you cooking me tonight?"

She took a step back and he inhaled a breath of relief, until her next move sucked the wind back out.

Reaching behind her, she began unzipping her sundress. "I don't cook."

"But I thought—"

"I asked you to dinner. I never said I was going to make it." The sound of her zipper sliding down her back was the only thing louder than the thump of his heart. "The pizza guy's coming in an hour and a half."

Then she nudged the dress off her shoulders and let it fall to the floor. Underneath was the sexiest example of the human form he'd ever seen, all wrapped up in a lacy blue bustier and matching thong. Sleek, silky legs seemed to stretch for miles, her navel was pierced, adorned with a single blue topaz, but it was the cleavage that snagged his attention like a glistening pot of gold.

His heart pumped faster, his cock swelled and his hands fisted at his sides. He didn't know what to sample first. Her body was like an expansive buffet set out before a sex-starved male. Question was would he be the one to feast or be feasted? The look in her eyes said it could go either way.

"And as for dessert," she said, "I'm one of those people who prefer it before dinner."

She slid up against him and he almost feared her touch. He'd wanted to remain a Southern gentleman, at least for a date or two, but with one brush of her lips to his neck, one caress of her hands to his chest, she'd reduced him to his most primal animal form. His mouth returned to hers, his hands found their way to her ass, and when he squeezed those silky cheeks, every ounce of civility drained from his blood.

He'd gone back to that caveman state, his hot hardened body fighting the urge to pick her up and drag her off to his den. But when she grabbed his hand and nudged him toward the hall, he realized he didn't have to.

His primal mate was already leading the way.

6

NICOLE WASN'T ABOUT TO let anything interfere with her plans for Devon tonight. Eighteen months. She'd counted. Eighteen months since she'd last been with a man. No wonder her insides turned to flames every time she came near him. Her tank was clearly on empty, running on fumes, ready to ignite with the slightest spark. That had to be it, had to be the reason she'd stripped naked in front of the man before he could even finish his drink.

Okay, so she had planned that he would catch a glimpse of her new lingerie, she'd just expected it to happen a little later. She hadn't thought a mere kiss would have her skipping the preliminaries and rushing to Act Two before the curtain came down. And the way she felt right now, even this wasn't happening fast enough. In her hurried attempt to get Devon into the bedroom and out of his clothes, his belt got stuck, his shoes wouldn't slip off, and how many damn buttons did they have to put on this shirt, anyway?

Shrugging out of his sports jacket, he let it fall

to the floor then moved to help her with the shirt, probably noting the look of frustration in her eyes.

"I want you *now*," she said, realizing too late that she'd said it out loud. She hadn't wanted to sound so desperate, yet there was something about the man that brought it out of her.

Yanking open the last two buttons, he pulled off his shirt. "That won't be a problem," he said, then he took her in his arms and claimed her mouth with his.

He cupped her cheek in one hand and held her against him with the other, exposing his chest in all its glory, pressed against her breasts like a pulsing mound of stone. His woodsy scent encased her and she let herself fall against him, to drown in his embrace and feed on the sensation of his touch. His tongue circled hers, telling in no uncertain terms the many ways that tongue could pleasure her, and a guttural moan slipped from her throat as she considered each one.

She brushed her hands up his back wanting to feel every inch of the sinewy flesh, to replace what she'd imagined with the reality in her arms. Pressing her waist against his groin she felt his cock jerk and harden when she squeezed a hand to his ass, and her stomach fluttered at the thought that she'd found an erogenous zone. She wanted to know everything that turned him on, how he liked to be touched, his weaknesses, his delights, and what kinds of things could reduce him to a shuddering, sated mass.

"I think I need you horizontal," he whispered.

Tugging against his trousers, she replied, "I think I need you naked."

Like a willing captor obeying a command, he tossed them off then kicked them aside with one foot, and when she took a step back, she found herself staring at six feet of perfection.

The man was long and lean, with hair in just the right places and bulk where it belonged. Nicole lowered her eyes to one impressive erection. She couldn't stop herself panting in anticipation.

Her body swelled with desire, the new bustier turning to a vise against her breasts, the thong a tight belt at her waist. She wanted to be as unobstructed as her mate, but before she could move to pull the lingerie off, Devon whisked her into his arms and deposited her on the bed. The sweet look of affection in his eyes had darkened to steamy need, and when he grabbed the scraps of fabric and pulled them off, she knew this particular encounter would be everything she'd hoped.

"Condoms," she said, pointing to the bedside table, but Devon moved to his pants instead, rummaging through the pockets and cursing under his breath before coming up with the foil packet.

He sheathed his length and moved back to the bed, and the hot rise of arousal swept through her. She couldn't wait to take him in and feel his impending release, and holding out her arms, she urged him on top of her.

Instead, he stood at the edge and pulled her closer to him, leaning over her but keeping his feet on the floor. He brought his lips close to hers and gazed into her eyes, brushing a stray hair from her face with the tip of his thumb.

"You're so beautiful," he said, the depth in his tone touching something inside. It was the seriousness in his eyes, the layers of emotion on his face that told her there was more to the statement than those words, and if it were possible to get any hotter, she'd just crossed over into molten.

Her clit swelled with need, her breasts ached, her heart pounded, and when she ran her hands over his dense, rigid chest, he moved down and took her in his arms.

"I need you," she groaned, squirming against him, his hard cock wedged between them, taunting her, sending the ache even deeper. His eyes never leaving hers, he tucked one arm under her knee and raised her leg over his shoulder.

"You drive me crazy," he said, the sharpness in his voice telling her he was as tight for release as she. Then he brought his mouth to hers and slipped his shaft between her folds, brushing over her slick heat but not venturing inside. Her clit pulsed against his touch and he moaned, his chest vibrating against hers, his mouth devouring her mewling pleas.

She couldn't catch her breath. The ache between her legs had swelled to a throb, and when he slid his cock over her again, she pulled her mouth from his and whispered, "You're killing me."

His evil smile said that's what he'd intended. The man was teasing her, torturing her, and the fact that he had the strength to hold back turned her need to fury.

She wiggled under him then grabbed her hands onto his ass and squeezed; that newfound weakness was all it took to rip the smile from his lips and toss him toward the edge. He buried his face in the crook of her neck and groaned, his cock twitching between her legs before he pulled his hips back, rose up and drove himself inside.

Every muscle in her body went limp with the glorious feel of him stretching her, filling her, until he'd buried himself completely.

"Oh," he groaned. "This is going to go fast."

"I don't need time," she pressed, curving her back to take him deeper inside.

Almost involuntarily, he began pumping inside her, his eyes fixed on hers, his face taking on more color with every thrust.

"Too fast," he said, and even that seemed an effort to expel. His eyes had glazed over with need, the propriety stripped from his facade so that what she saw was the inner workings of a man driven with desire.

She dug her fingers into his ass and pulled him closer, a rippling sensation running through her, marking the start of an orgasm that threatened to rip through her with one more thrust.

He pulled out then pushed in again, out and in until the searing bolt of pleasure tore through her with a scream.

Convulsing under him, her body fisted hard around him. White light blinded her, a high-pitched whine deafened her, and before the fog cleared, Devon threw her other leg over his shoulder and cried out as he poured his climax inside.

Their bodies moved without will, thrusting and jerking, clasping and contracting until a wave of silken pleasure smoothed over and she collapsed against the bed.

Devon's bare chest thumped hard against her. His breath came out in grunts. And before his weight bore down on her, he pulled out and fell onto his back beside her.

Nicole didn't know what to say. That was the most intense orgasm she'd ever had, and just as she found the strength to say so, Devon interrupted.

"Wow. Can we do that again?"

A breathy chuckle broke her silence and she lay on her back staring at the ceiling.

"Yeah," she said. "I'd like to do that again."

"I HAVE TO ADMIT, I've never had dinner in bed," Devon said, taking a bite of the sausage and olive pizza Nicole had ordered.

She swallowed and added, "I don't think I've ever had pizza naked."

They'd climbed under the covers and had flicked

on the television in her bedroom. She'd thrown a DVD in the player and they dined while Vito Corleone danced at his daughter's wedding in the opening scenes of *The Godfather*. A bottle of red wine rounded out what Devon considered to be an evening just short of perfection. It could only be improved if this was a hotel room and they were on a week-long vacation, not to be disturbed for at least seven more days.

He'd already concluded a simple taste of this woman wouldn't be nearly enough. Already, his mind was conjuring up the different ways he'd like to explore her mind and body, to push her back to that screaming, writhing frenzy and implant that sated smile on her lips for good. Just the thought made his cock twitch with expectation.

Unfortunately, it was Wednesday. Life would come sneaking up before they knew it, and he wondered how quickly he could talk Nicole into getting away for a more extended period of time. He definitely wanted more than this one night. A lifetime would be good. But for the moment, he'd settle for a weekend.

"That's the part where you're supposed to say, me neither."

Devon blinked from his thoughts. "Huh?"

"Eating pizza naked. You look like you're trying to recall whether you've done that before." She smiled and laughed. "Were your college years a little wilder than mine?"

"No," he said, pulling the blankets up around

his chest and scooting closer. "My mind drifted to what a wonderful time I'm having tonight. I mean, for a guy, this is about as good as life gets."

She crinkled that turned-up nose and smiled. "Really?"

"Are you kidding?" he scoffed. "Pizza and *The Godfather* while naked in bed with a beautiful blonde? Men have started wars over less."

She pulled another slice of pizza from the box between them then grabbed the bottle of wine and filled her glass. "I suppose when you put it that way," she said. "I'd say I was too lazy to get dressed and too relaxed to leave the bedroom. And as far as the movie, well, it's been one of my favorites for years."

"I wouldn't have considered *The Godfather* a chick flick."

She frowned. "Not all chicks are crazy about chick flicks. We do like some of the classics, you know." Gesturing toward the TV, she added, "I used to be in love with Michael Corleone when I was a kid. I wanted to be his wife."

Devon raised a brow. "Which one? The one that got blown up in the car or the one he estranged from her children after the divorce?"

She laughed. "Okay, so maybe I hadn't wished that in the literal sense." She reached for her wineglass and snuggled closer. "I think it's the glamour, the wealth, the danger, all underscored by their deep sense of family. I don't know. I think there's something romantic about it all." She smirked and added, "All that money certainly doesn't hurt."

"Not exactly spoken like a woman who's about to become a millionaire."

For a moment, the comment hung in the air until Nicole sighed and shrugged. "I don't know if we're really going to see the money, and if we do, I don't expect it to change my life much."

"You don't plan to go out and buy a bunch of fancy toys?"

She shook her head. "Not really. When it comes to material things, I'm pretty happy with what I've got."

"So what *do* you plan to do with the money?"

She tossed her pizza crust in the box and waved it off when he offered more, prompting him to move the box to the floor. Taking a sip of his wine, he decided he'd had enough dinner for the night and was ready to move on to dessert anyway.

She leaned over and set her wine on the bedside table, then moved back into his arms, settling her head against his chest and easing into his embrace. A smooth sense of comfort came over him, a relaxed feeling of contentment that seemed to come so readily when he was with her, and he wondered if this was the stuff that made a woman a soul mate.

It sure felt like it.

"I've been trying to figure that out for a while now," she said. "I really don't want to just buy a lot of expensive things. I'd like to know that the money ended up doing something good for someone."

"Are you thinking about setting up a charity foundation?"

"Probably, if I can't get more creative than that, but I don't know. There are so many charities, so many worthy causes it's hard deciding who gets what. A person could spend their life just doing the research and doling out the funds. And when it's all said and done, I keep feeling there's a group of people being left behind."

"Like?"

"Like maybe those who are stuck between having too much money to qualify for financial aid but not enough to really survive. You know, people who, if they had a little extra help, it would mean all the difference in the world. Maybe a college fund for their kids, or a down payment on a home of their own. I don't know, but I kind of like the idea of setting up something of my own that's very up close and personal."

She looked up at him with those beautiful blue eyes, prompting him to tease, "I can think of a number of charitable causes that could benefit by having you up close and personal."

"Really," she said, flicking a brow. "Are you trying to tell me you're needy?"

Reaching for the remote control, he pressed the button to shut off the television, then moved back and cupped her cheek. "I'm most definitely a worthy cause, but it's not your money I'm after."

Slowly and softly he tasted her lips, enjoying the

casual warmth as it simmered in his veins. So far they'd only succumbed to frenzied passion, heat that rose too quickly and fire that spread too fast. They'd needed to take the edge off, and now that they had, he was ready to come back around at a more temperate pace, savoring the journey instead of rushing toward the end.

He shifted and settled her back against the pillows, making her comfortable for the long road ahead. He wanted to sample every inch of her, explore every curve, and when she smiled and exhaled a breath of calm agreement, he knew he'd be granted the luxury of doing just that.

He slid his fingers through her long silky hair while he kissed her, soaking in the rich essence of the red wine, circling his tongue with hers and then moving his mouth to the tender flesh below her chin. She let her head sink into the pillows while he made his way down the curve of her neck, across her shoulder and down to one breast, and when he took that hard nipple into his mouth, her gasp of pleasure flooded him with a rush of heat.

He licked her nipple then let his breath warm the bud as he whispered, "I can't get enough of these."

She caressed her slim fingers through his hair and arched her back to greet him, pulling him closer, telling him she liked his touch and wanted him hard and strong. He let his teeth graze her skin and she let out a groan that sprung his cock to attention. This was supposed to go slowly, but damn if his body didn't have other ideas. He'd barely touched her and already the strain was growing, pulling the blood from his head and rushing it to his loins.

He turned dizzy with lust as he suckled one breast and teased the other between his fingers, and with this woman in his arms all sense of time and space quickly disappeared. It was just him and these breasts, small but full, and with the right amount of pout to fill his mouth with joy. He moved from one to the other, relishing the taste of her and the flowery scent of her skin. Smoothing a hand down her waist, he circled a thumb over the tiny stone in her navel and moaned. She was ridiculously sexy, and he wanted her now. Tomorrow. Forever.

Desire rushed through him like wildfire, stiffening his cock and tensing his muscles, and underneath him, Nicole began to writhe and shiver, telling him her lust poured as richly as his. She rocked up and down as he migrated south, along the taut expanse of her waist to that sexy topaz he wanted to take in his mouth.

Tapping his shoulder, she'd produced a condom, and he met her eyes and smiled. "Later," he said, his voice raspy and low.

The room growing hot, he sat up and tossed the blankets over the foot of the bed then straddled her and studied the stunning beauty he'd captured. Her body splayed open, her cheeks bright pink and those yellow tresses fanned around her face, she looked like a golden angel, but her wicked look of need said she was anything but.

Quirking a brow, he smiled. "I've got a spot I'd like to revisit," he said, positioning himself in front of her slick, wet heat. The scent of sex turned him harder, snatching his breath and pounding a beat against his chest. He slowly slid his hands along her thighs and she opened herself to him, spreading eagerly for him, and the raw power he held encased him. She bit her lip, once, twice, three times, her eyes pleading with need as he teased his thumbs around her folds.

Up close and personal, he thought. This was exactly where he wanted her, her sex in his hands, against his mouth, swelling and pulsing, and when he gently touched her curls and took the nub between his lips, her aching cry nearly causing him to lose control.

She arched into him and cupped his head in her hands, pulling him closer and reacting to the rhythm of his tongue. Her low hum encouraged him, filling his ears with her lovely sound of pleasure, and when he slipped a finger inside, the tone lowered to a breathy, "Yes."

He loved that she wasn't shy about what she wanted and how easily he could read her needs. Taking the guesswork out of sex left him free to peruse and explore, and when he slipped a second finger inside, she responded with a deep sultry, "Ohhhh."

He groaned into her clit, pushing his fingers in and out, circling his tongue around the nub until she squirmed under him and called out, "Now. Now." She held out the condom, but he pushed it aside.

"Not yet, baby," he said. "I want you to come in my mouth."

"But—" she said, and the objection drowned with a gurgle when he sucked her clit into his mouth and lapped against it.

"Oh," she moaned, the sound more a warning than cry of pleasure, and when she began to wiggle underneath him, he pulled his fingers from her and steadied her thighs.

She groaned again, this time with more urgency, and as her clit swelled against his tongue, he knew the next sound in his ears would be a guttural cry of release.

Slick heat soaked his chin, her salty scent drugged his senses, and the farther she moved toward the edge, the harder he held her in place. Her hips thrust and gyrated, the nub pulsed against his tongue. She tried to squirm out from under him, but he dug his fingers into her thighs and held her tight. He needed this, needed the sensation of her release against his tongue, and when he heard her suck in a sharp breath, she shattered in his arms.

Her cry echoed through the room, her clit convulsed between his lips, searing a bolt through his cock that tightened his balls and nearly stopped his heart. He'd never come without direct stimulation, but when she shrieked his name and churned against him, his own orgasm rushed to be answered.

Out of necessity, he broke his hold on her and rose to his knees in time to watch her collapse against the bed, every muscle in her body giving out to the weight of her release. Wisps of silky hair fell haphazardly across her face. Her skin rosy, her lips puffed, and when she opened her eyes and glanced up at him her look of total pleasure tore something deep inside him.

The woman was insanely beautiful, and in that moment he knew the vision he was staring at was the vision he wanted to wake up to every day. This was something special, something real, and when her mouth curved into a smile, his heart smiled with her.

She loosely waved the condom in front of him and asked, "Are you ready for it now?"

Snatching the foil pack in mid-air, he nodded.

"Oh, yeah. I'm ready."

7

"YOU GOT SOME, didn't you?"

Nicole stared blankly at Eve. "Got what?"

Pulling from the doorway, Eve stepped into Nicole's office and leaned a hip against her desk. "Oh, please. Look at you. You have 'I got laid' written all over your face."

Nicole's cheeks heated up. She tried to scoff but a smile leaked through, ruining the effect. She always had been a horrible poker player.

"I don't know what you're talking about," she attempted, not exactly sure she wanted her love life advertised around the station. Although this *was* Eve, and Nicole *was* dying to tell someone about the great evening she'd had.

"Uh-huh," Eve said. "Like we've ever heard you whistling before."

"Whistling?"

"Whistling. 'What's Love Got To Do With It', if I'm not mistaken."

Nicole hadn't realized she could carry that good a tune, but Eve nailed it.

"That and I overheard you say good morning to Ray on your way in."

"So I said good morning to Ray. Big deal."

"It is a big deal considering you stopped acknowledging the man when he started hitting on you last fall."

"I wasn't interested and he was relentless. I couldn't afford to give him mixed signals."

"But you can now?"

Nicole shrugged.

"Oh, and let's not forget about this," Eve said, holding the expense account Nicole had turned into accounts payable this morning. Eve turned the stapled group of papers to one particular receipt and handed it to Nicole. "Since when does the station buy lingerie for its employees?"

"Uh, that shouldn't be there. It must have gotten stuck to the others."

Eve smiled. "A satin bustier and thong set, huh?"

"Look, I happened to be there researching our summer bridal show. Penny and I had been to a dozen bridal boutiques. I was hungry, my feet were killing me and I felt I deserved a present." She yanked the receipt off the stack, double-checked the others then handed the papers back to Eve. "That's all there was to it."

"And how did Devon like it?"

The quirky look on Eve's face finally caused Nicole to break down and laugh. "Okay, okay. I give up. If you must know, the bustier and the thong are lying in shreds on my bedroom floor." Holding up the receipt, she added, "This was a short-lived eighty-five dollars."

"But worth every cent?"

"Oh, yeah."

Eve looked her up and down. "I like the new you. I hope it lasts."

"I don't see why it wouldn't."

"So when are you seeing him again?"

Nicole pushed back and relaxed in her chair, trying to recall Devon's exact words. "He's taking me to some family dinner next weekend, but I'm sure I'll be seeing him before then. He said he'd call."

Eve's eyes widened. "He's taking you home to meet the parents?"

Nicole frowned. "No. Well, yes. I guess. He didn't exactly word it like that. It's a family dinner and he wants me to come."

"He wants you to meet Mom and Dad."

"Okay, so what?"

"So it sounds to me like he's serious about you."

Nicole waved her off. "Don't be silly. We've only been on a couple dates. This thing isn't serious at all."

"Does *he* know that?"

"Of course, he knows that." At least, she hoped he did. She shook her head. No, *of course* he did. He hadn't given her the slightest sign that what they had was anything more than a fling.

Then she noticed the long stem roses that took up her entire credenza and her frown deepened.

"No," she resolved. "We're light years from serious. This is only a fling, and a very good one at that."

"It looks like it," Eve said. "You look...healthy."

Nicole relaxed and laughed. "I feel healthy. In fact, I think casual sex should be prescribed as part of every woman's weekly regimen." She paused and tapped her pencil to her lips. "Now, there's an idea for a segment. The spiritual benefits of non-committal sex from a biological standpoint. You know, like a form of wellness. Like Yoga or meditation."

"Way to make your love life sound like a multi-vitamin."

She shrugged. "Maybe it is, in a way. I know I haven't felt better in years. I think women would be better off if we stopped looking at sex as a path to love and started thinking of it as part of a well-rounded lifestyle. We should be having fun exploring what turns us on and enjoying the moment like men do instead of constantly turning every date into something serious."

"Well, I can't argue with that. I've sometimes thought men had healthier views about sex than women."

Nicole scribbled the idea on her pad, thinking it was well worth considering. Given her situation and all the issues in her life, she wasn't anywhere near thinking about marriage and family. She needed to figure out who she was first, then figure out what she wanted in a partner.

And last night with Devon had made strides where that was concerned. It was the first time she'd ever been with a man and just enjoyed the physical act of sex—and boy did she enjoy it. There was definitely something liberating in letting go of tomorrow and enjoying today, exploring the soul and body without overanalyzing the situation or wondering where it all was heading. And she intended to make this new attitude her habit.

This was exactly what she needed at this point in her life. And she had to believe there were thousands of other women out there feeling the same way, looking to find their own way in life without letting a man take the wheel and do the steering.

"I'll check into this idea and maybe bring it up in our next meeting," Nicole said, then glanced down to her watch. "But in the meantime, I've got an appointment with an investigator."

"An investigator?" Eve said, curling the expense report into a tube and pushing off the desk.

"For the segment, 'Know Your Mate Before It's Too Late'. He runs a service that provides background checks on prospective lovers. You know, to make sure the person you're sleeping with isn't wanted in several states."

"That's right," Eve said, tapping the papers in her

hand. "That's going to be a good segment. There are strong opinions on both sides of that debate."

"I've already secured Nancy Shepard, the woman who hooked up with that con artist who bilked her out of thirty grand. We've got the author who wrote the book *Must We Trust* where he talks about this new trend of couples checking each other out before taking the plunge. I hadn't realized how deeply he'd studied the subject, how people in other cultures court, and how embedded blind trust is into the way men and women come together. Lots of people are really put off by the idea of a date checking up on them, but the ones who've been burned tell a pretty convincing story."

Eve leaned against the threshold and stared for a moment. "I don't know if I could do that—run a background check on a guy I just met. It feels like snooping."

"Well, I could. I think people have a right to know who they're dealing with, and if you haven't got anything to hide, what's the problem?"

Of course, two years ago she probably would have sided with Eve. Before her parents had been forced to tell her the truth about her birth she believed in the idea of protecting a person's privacy. Particularly with the Internet making private information public, it seemed a person's private life was open to anyone with a computer and a credit card.

She'd felt people had a right to their secrets, until it occurred to her that one person's secret could be another person's identity. Her parents had felt her adoption was no one's business, and so it had been a tightly held secret among their closest friends and family.

A number of people had known about it. After all, a woman didn't just show up with a newborn without raising questions. But Don and Betty wanted the world to think Nicole was their blood child and the people around them helped them do that. If it hadn't been bad enough to discover she wasn't who she thought she was, it was worse to find out other people knew about it and kept their mouths shut.

And that was right about the time Nicole changed her views on privacy. Granted, she hadn't walked into Atlanta telling everyone why she was here. These people were friends and coworkers who had no stake in what she'd come here to do. But when it came to family and relationships, the notion of keeping secrets left a bitter taste in her mouth, and if there were services out there to tell the truth when people wouldn't, then more power to them.

"Still," Nicole said, "I think the debate will be good for the show."

"So what's the investigator bringing to the table?"

"He's got some interesting stories to tell about background checks he's provided. Although, his opinion will be slanted in favor of his business. If something ended badly, he's not likely to tell us about it. We'll have to balance our story with the other perspective, and Penny's working on that. In the meantime, I'm going ahead and ordering background checks on me and Devon just for kicks. It will be interesting to see for myself what information pops up, how I'd feel about someone reading what's in mine, and how I feel about what I find in Devon's."

Eve flicked her brows. "Checking up on the new fling, huh?"

Nicole scoffed. "This is purely for the show, but I'll tell you, given the millions we might be walking into, we should probably keep this guy's card. And we have to be even more careful than the rest of them given the fact that our names have been splashed all over the news. You never know what kind of con artists could be coming out of the woodwork."

"Speaking of news, did you get a call from *The Globe?*" Eve asked. "Zach and I both did."

"Yeah," she said. "I told them no comment like we all agreed," adding, "I'll be happy when this craziness is over." And she meant it. She'd like nothing more than to settle the suit so she could move on with her life.

"Yes, let's hope Jenna comes up with good news soon. I checked in with her the other day, but she didn't have anything new. She still believes Liza has a weak case, so that's promising."

Nicole nodded. "We should pray that situation doesn't change."

"HOW ARE YOU HOLDING up?" Devon asked, handing Nicole a glass of wine.

"Fine," she said, a little too quickly. "Your parents are very nice, very comfortable to be around."

Which had come as a relief. When they'd driven through the large iron gates and parked in front of what looked more like the White House than somebody's home, her stomach had done a flip-flop. She knew how wealthy families could be, particularly ones labeled "old money," and she feared an evening of boredom and high brow scrutiny.

What she got was anything but.

Take away the expensive jewelry and palatial estate and one would never guess this was anything but an average working class family. Devon's mother, Carol Anne, a petite, almost pixie-like woman, seemed more fitted for a church bake sale than the stuffy investor dinners they'd described. The woman chatted incessantly; her wide-eyed interest in her children's lives the only thing letting the rest of them get a word in edgewise. Her husband, William, stood a full foot taller and though Nicole could see the shrewd businessman behind those stark blue eyes, at home he clearly relinquished control to his wife and children.

And Nicole couldn't blame him. Between Todd and Grace warring for attention as the respective baby and only girl in the family, Bryce's sour wit, Devon's dry humor and their mother talking over the entire crew, there wasn't much left for anyone else.

Dinner at the Bradshaws was pretty much an orchestra of four boisterous grown children, led by their mother the maestro, and everyone else in the room was relegated to the balcony.

"Everyone's very nice," she added, backing it up with a smile.

"They're all nuts," he said, taking a seat on the couch next to her.

After dinner, they'd announced dessert would be served in the front parlor, though so far Devon and Nicole were the only two who'd migrated. Grace and Carol had begun clearing the table, despite the fact that they had servers handling the meal. Todd had disappeared with his date, a woman named Chenille, whom Devon cautioned her not to get attached to. Apparently Todd's dates revolved as fast as the doors at Macy's during a summer clearance sale. William and Bryce were last seen still sitting at the dinner table, talking stocks with Grace's husband, Brad.

For the time being, it was only Nicole and Devon, and she had to admit appreciation for the moment of peace.

"They aren't nuts," she said, though she couldn't manage the remark with the right amount of seriousness on her face. Truth was they *were* nuts, but in a good way, a way that put you at ease. Around Devon's family, you could be slightly dysfunctional and still fit right in. They may all be bright and successful, but each one was flawed enough to keep them real.

She shifted toward him as he wrapped an arm around her shoulder. "So...with servers taking care of the dinner, why is your mom clearing the plates?" she asked.

"Mom's completely blue collar, grew up in a small town called Mud Tavern, Alabama. She'll never get used to people picking up after her, so she helps the staff."

"That's kind of nice."

"They hate her."

Nicole nearly choked on her wine. "Why?"

Devon shrugged the comment off. "Mom can't grasp the fact that these people want to do their jobs and go home. She thinks they're family, and when she's in the kitchen, she thinks she's helping."

"But she's not."

"They can't get anything done." He glanced at his watch. "Dad will give her another five minutes then call her out of there. It's the deal he struck to keep them from quitting. Let her help for a few minutes then get her the hell out so they can finish up and go home to their real families."

She tried not to giggle. "They really threatened to quit?"

"Would you like my mother in your office while you're trying to work?"

The giggle escaped and she shook her head.

"You're still here." Bryce walked into the spacious room and took a seat in one of the leather club chairs. "Our guests usually go AWOL as soon as they're freed from the dinner table."

She winced. "Oh, you aren't *that* bad."

"He's kidding," Devon said.

"Wait until you see Christmas with the extended family," Bryce said. "You'll change your mind."

Devon squeezed a hand on her shoulder as if to agree, and a sudden discomfort came over her. Eve's words came back to her, the remarks about meeting Devon's parents and things getting serious between them. She'd dismissed them before, and her sensible side told her to dismiss them now. It was a silly off-handed comment about the holidays, not a proposal for marriage, but the heavy feeling in her gut said Devon might be taking things more seriously than he should. Her head wasn't in the right place for anything more than casual friendship, and for the second time, she wondered if she should make that clear.

Or was she simply being overly sensitive?

"It's not fair." Grace waltzed into the room with Todd on her heels, the two apparently in the midst of a disagreement. Brad and Chenille followed, both looking as though they'd like to be anywhere but in this house right now.

"Grandma Mayberry said that locket was mine," Todd said.

"You're a guy. What are you going to do with a silver locket?"

"I could have a daughter someday, you know."

Devon pulled Nicole close. "Care for a tour of the gardens?"

Before Nicole could answer, Devon's parents slipped in.

"Marilyn made her special red velvet cake," Carol said, then turned to Nicole. "Do you like red velvet cake?"

Nicole nodded even though she had no idea what it was.

"We're just waiting for the coffee."

"Mom," Todd said. "Grandma promised me that locket."

"What locket, dear?"

"The silver one with the picture inside of her holding you as a baby. She'd always wanted me to have it because she said I looked just like you when I was born."

"That's absurd. She said the same thing about Bryce but you don't see him hoarding all grandma's jewelry over it," Grace argued.

"I'm not hoarding the jewelry. I want the locket grandma promised me."

Devon cleared his throat. "Why are we talking about this now?"

"The will," Todd said. "Mom and dad are updating the will and mom asked if there's anything special we want to make sure we get when they're gone. I told her I wanted the locket and brat here had a cow."

"There's four of us and we should all be discuss-

ing this together, some other day, when we don't
have company," Grace said.

"Now, there's a gathering I can't wait for,"
Bryce mocked.

As the two continued to argue, Nicole remembered some of the heirlooms her family had. Her
middle class family didn't have much, which made
what they did have all that more precious.

Their great grandfather's watch would surely go
to Nate, and she'd always assumed she'd get
Grandma Dorothy's pearls. But did any of those
things really belong to her now? Surely, there were
cousins more deserving, blood relations who should
come before a girl adopted into the family.

Nicole knew her parents would reject that attitude.
They'd tell her she had every right to the things they
passed on to her, that she was their daughter in every
way that mattered. So why couldn't she accept that?

She wondered who her real parents were,
whether they had a token or a small heirloom
they'd been holding for her in the event she
someday returned. Did they have a photo of her
as a newborn? Did she hold a place in their
hearts? And how would she feel if she discovered
she didn't?

These were all the questions she'd come here to
sort out, but in the nine months she'd been here,
she'd barely made progress. Okay, she'd used the job
as an excuse, and the moment that began to settle
she'd turned her focus to the lottery and then to

Devon, telling herself she deserved this temporary break. But was this really a break or was she only looking for a new excuse to avoid moving forward?

Her throat began to thicken as she looked around the room. It wasn't unlike her own parents' living room, much larger, but the feeling was the same. And so was Devon's family. She only had her brother, Nate, but he'd been everything to her, until she discovered he was Don and Betty's natural child and she wasn't. That fact had driven a stake in her heart, threw a bitter wedge between them that she didn't want. Not outwardly, but deep inside. It was part of the reason she left California. The more time she spent with Nate, the greater chance he had at seeing the resentment she'd begun to harbor, and she didn't want to do anything that might damage their relationship for good. She'd needed to distance herself from all of them, to sort things out in her head before she took a bad situation and made it all worse.

She didn't want to live with this confusion. She wanted to be whole again. She wanted to let go of all the hurt and go back to life like it was before, but the pain wouldn't let her.

Being with Devon felt good—really good. He made her forget, made her feel like the woman she used to be, until gatherings like these reminded her how messed up her life really was.

She looked around the room at a family in love, despite their disagreements. They may be crazy and eccentric, but the bond between them was clear,

The Harlequin Reader Service® — Here's how it works:

Accepting your 2 free books and 2 free gifts places you under no obligation to buy anything. You may keep the books and gifts and return the shipping statement marked "cancel". If you do not cancel, about a month later we'll send you 6 additional books and bill you just $3.99 each in the U.S. or $4.47 each in Canada, plus 25¢ shipping & handling per book and applicable taxes if any.* That's the complete price and — compared to cover prices of $4.75 each in the U.S. and $5.75 each in Canada — it's quite a bargain! You may cancel at any time, but if you choose to continue, every month we'll send you 6 more books which you may either purchase at the discount price or return to us and cancel your subscription.

*Terms and prices subject to change without notice. Sales tax applicable in N.Y. Canadian residents will be charged applicable provincial taxes and GST. Credit or debit balances in a customer's account(s) may be offset by any other outstanding balance owed by or to the customer. Please allow 4 to 6 weeks for delivery. Offer available while quantities last.

If offer card is missing write to: Harlequin Reader Service, 3010 Walden Ave., P.O. Box 1867, Buffalo NY 14240-1867

NO POSTAGE
NECESSARY
IF MAILED
IN THE
UNITED STATES

BUSINESS REPLY MAIL
FIRST-CLASS MAIL   PERMIT NO. 717   BUFFALO, NY

POSTAGE WILL BE PAID BY ADDRESSEE

HARLEQUIN READER SERVICE
3010 WALDEN AVE
PO BOX 1867
BUFFALO NY 14240-9952

Play the Lucky Hearts Game

and get...

2 FREE BOOKS and
2 FREE MYSTERY GIFTS...

yes! YOURS to KEEP!

I have scratched off the silver card.
Please send me my *2 FREE BOOKS* and
2 FREE mystery GIFTS. I understand that I
am under no obligation to purchase any books
as explained on the back of this card.

Scratch Here!
then look below to see
what your cards get you...
2 Free Books & 2 Free
Mystery Gifts!

351 HDL ENSL   151 HDL ENZL

FIRST NAME

LAST NAME

ADDRESS

APT.#

CITY

STATE/ PROV.

ZIP/POSTAL CODE

(H-B-08/07)

Twenty-one gets you
2 FREE BOOKS and
2 FREE MYSTERY GIFTS!

Twenty gets you
2 FREE BOOKS!

Nineteen gets you
1 FREE BOOK!

TRY AGAIN!

and that realization brought a swell of tears to her eyes.

She lowered her gaze and spoke to Devon's lap. "I would like some air," she said, rising and moving toward the large French doors before he had a chance to object.

She felt the need to flee, to start running and not stop until her mind went blank and her body collapsed from exhaustion. It was an old familiar feeling she'd grown tired of, and she wondered if she'd ever lose it for good.

This visit had been a mistake. She shouldn't have come here, but Devon had made her forget. He'd given her that temporary respite that made her think life had gone back to normal, when it was anything but.

She pulled on the handle and stepped onto the side patio, gulping in the warm afternoon air, trying to calm the pounding in her chest and quell the wetness in her eyes. She took four steps toward the woodsy perimeter of the property then turned toward the back of the estate where the gardens looked quiet and the tree line thickened into dense woods.

"Nicole, are you okay?" Devon called after closing the door and stepping up behind her.

"I, um…" she started, having no idea what to say. How should she explain her actions? What excuse could she give for standing up in front of his family and bolting for the door? They were all probably back there thinking she was emotionally unstable or something. And given the way she felt right now, she couldn't argue with the assumption.

"Honey," Devon said, pulling up beside her and wrapping an arm around her shoulder. "You're upset. Did someone say something to upset you?"

She shook her head, not wanting him to think his family had anything to do with her problems. They were nice people, fun and quirky and not at all to blame for her current mood. Which left her wondering what to say.

Maybe she could say she was homesick, or that dinner didn't agree with her.

She took five more steps toward the back yard, her mind racing for some plausible excuse for her actions, but the quicker she walked, the more it was clear that she should tell Devon the truth.

"What is it, babe?"

The look in his eyes was so sweet, so concerned. He really did care, and as a friend and lover he deserved an answer. But where to start?

They rounded the side yard and entered the large grassy garden that spanned the back of the property. A vast concrete patio ran from the house and circled a large swimming pool. Raised planter beds abutted two sides, creating a rock wall with a waterfall emptying into the deep end. More than one gazebo created seating among the flowers and trees, and at the far end of the patio stood a pool house the size of a small cottage.

Nicole made her way toward it for no other

reason than its distance from the house, her need for escape still running under her skin.

"Nic," he started, but she held up a hand to stop him then turned and stared into two worried blue eyes.

"I'm sorry," she said. "I didn't mean to up and leave like that. It was rude."

He shook his head. "I'm just concerned."

Swallowing the lump in her throat, she crossed her arms over her chest and gazed out into the woods. "Grace and Todd," she said. "Their conversation brought up some unpleasant feelings for me." She struggled for more words, her explanation not coming as easily as she'd hoped. "It has to do with my parents," she continued, "Don and Betty." Then she took a breath and blurted out, "I found out last year that they aren't my birth parents. I'd been adopted."

Holding her eyes on the trees beyond the grass, Devon's silence hung like a giant weight between them.

"I, uh…" he said, obviously not sure where to go from there, and the fact that he didn't immediately understand released the floodgates.

She looked him in the eye, the hurt in her chest turning to that old familiar anger. "They never told me, Devon. If I hadn't been standing in the doctor's office that day, I still wouldn't know. For twenty-eight years Don and Betty lied to me. They'd made me believe I was always theirs."

He spoke quietly. "I'm sorry."

"My mom had a hysterectomy. It was common knowledge, the reason they didn't have more children. She fought uterine cancer thirty years ago and survived, except all my life they'd told me it wasn't thirty years ago but twenty-five." She shook her head over the stupidity at how she uncovered the truth. "The doctor had made an off-handed comment. He'd said thirty years was a good run and he hoped this time her remission would give her another thirty more. I'd corrected him. I said twenty-five. It had been twenty-five years since she had uterine cancer. But I was the one corrected that day. My mother had had a hysterectomy all right, but it was three years before I was born, not two years after."

"Oh, babe," Devon groaned.

"Nate is theirs, but I'm not."

He took her in his arms and held her close, and she pressed her face to his chest, wanting to block it all out.

"If they'd told me as a child things would have been different. I wouldn't have grown up thinking I was something I'm not. But they didn't. They'd spent my lifetime leading me to believe I was their natural born child. They'd never given me the slightest clue. And then in one split second, when the doctor's words put that horror in their eyes, I knew he hadn't been mistaken. I wasn't their child and everything I knew to be true was ripped out from under me."

"Nicole, I'm so sorry," Devon said, brushing a hand down her hair and kissing the top of her head.

She pressed a cheek more tightly against his chest, a sense of relief washing over her as she confessed her situation. Since she'd come to Atlanta she hadn't talked much about it. She'd had her fill of talking back home. But for some reason, when it came to Devon, confessing her story felt like releasing a giant weight from her shoulders.

"I'm hurt and angry," she said. "But more than anything, I want my life back again. I'd tried dealing with all of this in California, talking it through with my parents, trying to understand why they did what they did. In their eyes, I am their daughter as if their blood ran through me. But I can't brush off the gaping hole this has left. It's like half of me is gone, and I don't know where to find it."

"Is that why you've come here?"

She nodded. "Apparently, this is where my birth family is, and at first, I'd thought if I found them, I'd complete the puzzle and be able to move on with my life."

"What did you find?"

She let out a faint chuckle. "I've barely started to look. Maybe it's fear. Maybe it's the feeling I'd be betraying Don and Betty. I thought I'd find the answers in this city, but since I've been in Atlanta all I've gotten is more confused."

"That's understandable."

Lifting her chin, she looked into his eyes. "I'm sorry I'm dumping all of this on you, in front of your family no less. The talk of family heirlooms and such sort of got to me." She wiped a stray tear from her cheek and swallowed back the others. "Being around you, I'd managed to bury the hurt and confusion, but sitting there with your family brought it all to the surface. I'm angry. And I don't know how to take the anger away."

He cupped her cheek in his hand and pressed his lips to hers. "Shhhh," he said. "Don't worry about them." Then he kissed her again, this time deeper, brushing his tongue over her lips and caressing away the pain.

She sank into the embrace, loving the way he always managed to erase the troubles from her thoughts and replace them with a sense of peace. She circled his tongue with hers and brushed her hands up his back then down, pressing her waist against the growing bulge.

He groaned in her mouth and pulled her closer, then whispered, "I'm sorry, Nic. I wish I could fix this for you."

Though he couldn't fix her for good, she knew he could definitely fix her for now. He touched his lips to her cheek, down her neck and up to the tender spot below her ear, draining the tension from her muscles and swelling desire between her thighs.

"I wish you could make love to me," she whispered, and the gaze in his eyes told her he agreed.

"The pool house," he said.

She moved her eyes to the cottage at his right. It looked to have been shut up for the winter, blinds closed over the windows and the planters at the entrance only now budding with young blooms.

"Won't they come looking?"

"They'll be busy yakking for hours."

And with a flick of his brow, he was off.

8

TAKING NICOLE'S HAND, Devon led her toward the door to the pool house and she noted his breath of relief when he tried the handle and found it unlocked. Glancing behind them, he pulled her inside then locked the door behind them.

She barely caught a glimpse of a cozy kitchen and back room before he led her through the space and over to a sitting room. Leather couches surrounded a slate coffee table, one side wall housing a big screen television and stereo system which no doubt controlled speakers throughout the back yard. At another time she'd stop and gawk, but right now the urgent need for Devon inside her overshadowed everything else, and when he came to rest on the couch and tugged her down on top of him, she lost all interest in the house.

Lifting her skirt, she came down over him, straddling his lap and taking his strong chin in her hands. "This is the best thing you can do for me," she said, before lowering her mouth to his.

His hands went to work unzipping the back of her dress then tugging it off her shoulders, exposing her breasts to his warm hungry hands. His touch soothed her, his mouth caressed hers, and while he gently fondled her nipples, she clasped him firmly and drank in his moans.

Off popped her bra and he quickly tossed it aside, bracing his hands against her ribs and lifting her breasts to his mouth. She gasped when he took one in, feeding on it like a man long past famished. She let her head fall back and she closed her eyes, concentrating on the feel of his tongue circling her nipple, his teeth grazing her breast, pushing more heat to her clit and draining the anger from her pores.

This was what she needed, these moments of total release, the abandonment of everything but this man's hands and body, pulling her back to the woman she once was. In Devon's arms she existed in lust, her body alive with need, her spirit purified by the fire he lit in her belly. Gone was the confusion, the sense of unease, replaced with good old unadulterated passion. It wasn't the answer to her problems. It didn't erase the issues she had to sort out, but it did give her a momentary respite, a place she could go to escape, if only for this little while.

She worked to unfasten his shirt buttons then spread the fabric off his shoulders and pressed her waist against his chest. She loved his chest, the muscled mass that contracted and contorted as he moved, the light dusting of hair that tickled her skin and swelled her insides. She loved feeling it against her, on top of her, or in the palms of her hands, and as she wriggled her navel against him, her pulse quickened.

He moved his mouth to her other breast and began feasting, the sensation rippling through her draining the moisture from her mouth and placing it between her legs. She squirmed with need, her clit swelling to an ache, and though his mouth was doing wonders, she needed him inside.

Lifting her skirt, she pulled aside the thong and guided his hand between her legs, enjoying the thrill of his deep groan when his fingers reached the slick heat between her folds. He pressed his mouth between her breasts and she cupped his head in her hands, kissing his forehead and arching her hips into his touch.

"You're so wet," he whispered. "And I'm really hard."

She giggled. "How handy." But her giggle transformed to a gasp when he brushed his thumb against her clit and slipped a finger inside.

"This has to go," he said, using his other hand to rip the thong from her waist, and when she was freed of all impediments, he went to work on his slacks, massaging her with one hand and exposing his stiff cock with the other.

Never releasing his grasp on her, he wriggled his wallet out of his pocket and produced a condom like a magician pulls a quarter from behind a kid's ear. She took the packet from his hand then sheathed his stiff length, her body throbbing from his touch and her fierce desire to get him inside.

Harder and harder he circled his thumb around her clit, slipping a second finger inside and bringing her to the brink of orgasm while he used his tongue to tease the flesh between her breasts.

"No," she said, pulling his hand away. "I want to come over your cock."

Lacing her fingers through his, she held them at his sides, hovering over him like a captor ready to take on its prey. Their eyes met, his blue pools deepening to something dark and erotic, and when she impaled her body on his thick shaft, he closed his eyes and swallowed as the sensation tore through him.

"Yes," she said. "That's what I want." And she began moving over him, pulling up then sinking back down, his body filling hers, closing the gap between her needs and desires, leaving her spirit whole for this brief moment of ultimate pleasure.

"I love watching you slide inside me," she said, pulling her dress over her head and tossing it to the ground. She lifted up so that the tip of his cock held just at the edge of her entrance then she used her fingers to part her folds, exposing the place where they joined, sinking slowly over him while they both watched his shaft disappear inside her core.

"That's so sexy," he groaned, the fiery look of arousal in his eyes feeding her desire to let go and take risks.

Up, she lifted, easing him out slowly then sliding back down, her clit twitching when it came in contact with the base of his shaft. Her body begged her to move faster, to pull and plunge them into a searing release, but this new feeling of control had become too arousing. She wanted to see where she could take it, how far she could push the limit before he lost it completely.

"I like to touch myself here," she said, shifting so she spread her folds with one hand and massaged her clit with the other. "Have you ever had a woman masturbate during sex?"

"No," he said in a voice hoarse with need. "I can do that," he added, motioning to take over for her, but she stopped him.

"Just watch me," she whispered, the guttural pleasure building like the beat of a distant drum. She moved slowly, taking him in, stretching for him then pulling out, her breath growing heavier as she stroked herself toward climax. From her chest came a low hum, and she went with it, allowing every part of her body to take over, dismissing any caution her mind might have tried to conjure.

Deeper she hummed until the sound took on more intent, the tone rising in unison to the sensation between her legs.

"I can't take much more," Devon warned, his eyes displaying a sense of depth and urgency she'd never seen before, and when he grunted as if to hold on, she allowed herself to let go.

The hum in her throat rose to a cry as she felt his shaft swell inside her. "Yes," she begged. "Come inside me. Come now."

He laced his hands around her neck and drew his mouth to hers as her body fell into abyss, drinking in her cries as she jerked and convulsed around him. Black heat numbed her senses of everything but the climax that sped up her spine and stiffened her limbs.

She braced her hands to his shoulders and quickened the pace, his face turning red against the pressure he tried to control.

"Take it in," he urged, pushing his cock deeper with every thrust, moving faster, growing bigger until a quick gasp told her he was there.

She clenched her muscles tightly around him, pulling up and sinking down, drawing out her own orgasm while she watched him succumb to his.

"Ah," he cried out, as he gripped her waist and held her steady while his hips jutted against hers. The sensation snatched the wind from her lungs, her body riding his wave as he bucked and jerked.

"Oh, Nic—oh," he groaned, spilling himself inside her.

In that moment they were one, hearts beating in rhythm, blood pulsing in tune. His breath was her breath, the line between them shattered, no way of telling where his spirit ended and hers began.

And there, Nicole felt total peace.

No past, no future, no needs and no responsibilities, just two souls moving together in this utopia of physical satisfaction. Somehow, he'd managed to reach in and pull out a woman she'd never seen. A woman she liked and hoped to see more of, and she couldn't help but wonder what else she'd find in the arms of Devon Bradshaw.

"I can't believe you tricked me into coming here," Nicole grumbled from her seat behind the visitor's dugout at Turner Field. "And the Braves are playing the Dodgers, no less."

"It was the only way I could get you to root for the Braves," Devon said. "Pitch them up against the Giants biggest rival."

"I'll admit, the only thing I find worse than the Braves would be the Dodgers. But I'm not rooting for anything more than a good game."

She took a bite of one very messy Bratwurst and attempted to lick her lips, but failed miserably. Ballpark dogs most definitely weren't the thing to eat if a girl was trying to impress a date by remaining quaint. Though she'd passed on the onions—hoping that sacrifice would come in handy later—she still had trouble keeping the mustard and sauerkraut in the bun where it belonged.

Using his napkin, Devon reached over and wiped a stray dot of mustard from the corner of her mouth, and it struck her how quickly the two had fallen into ease with each other.

"You have to admit, these are good dogs," he said.

She flashed him a reluctant grin before confessing, "Okay, I'll give you that." And with a sigh, she added, "And I'll admit this is a pretty nice ballpark."

"Pretty nice?"

"Work with me here. You've dragged an avid Giants fan to a Braves-Dodger game. Take what you can get, because this is all over the moment the crowd goes into its thirteenth round of the tomahawk chop."

He smiled. "You mean you'll give me the first twelve?"

"Only because it's a beautiful day and you're not bad to look at."

"Wow," he said, sitting back in his seat. "So many compliments. Be careful not to swell my ego."

Leaning in close, she whispered, "I have more fun swelling other parts of Devon Bradshaw."

"Easy, there's seven more innings in this game."

"We may only make a couple more, unless somewhere in this carnival there's a place to go for a quickie." Flicking a brow, she added, "How's the security in this place?"

"They'd make our park ranger look like a stand-up comedian."

"Ouch."

The pop of a bat drew their attention back to the game. Sitting behind the dugout, one had to keep an eye on foul balls that could come whipping past, but this particular hit was a high fly out to center field, easily caught by a player she didn't recognize.

"You know," Nicole said, "when you picked me

up in Gabe on this beautiful day with the top down, I'd thought for sure we were heading back out of town for a second try at that vista point."

Devon took a bite of his hot dog then washed it down with a gulp of soda. "I'd rather not spend my evening in a jail cell. Besides," he added with a frown, "I thought you liked baseball."

"I do," she replied. "And in all honesty, I am a little surprised I've been in Atlanta almost a year and have yet to come check out the park. Heck, even Nate's given me a hard time about that one."

"So why haven't you?"

Taking another bite of her bratwurst, she took the moment to consider then shrugged. "Too busy, I guess. And in a way, baseball was always kind of a family thing for me." She smiled at the thought. "Funny, how without my family around, I sort of lost interest in the game. And for my whole life, it was such a huge part of our upbringing."

She scanned the park, the familiar crisscross pattern of the outfield grass, the murmur of conversation that melded into a soothing, almost meditative hum. The malty smell of beer and the smoky aroma of barbecue, the echo of the announcer's voice calling over the loudspeakers. The warm soak of the afternoon sun on a bright spring day. All these things came together in that familiar feel of home, no matter what the venue or who was playing.

"All my life, my dad had season tickets. Four of them. It was the substitute for our annual vacation.

Mom, dad, Nate and me had gone to countless games dating back to the frigid days of Candlestick Park." She smiled and in her heart, she felt the tug of something loved and lost.

"Those were *really* the days, back in the eighties when the Giants sucked and the park was cold and horrible. We practically had the place to ourselves. And you can bet there weren't many corporate seats back in those days. Only real baseball fans came out to the park then, but for me, it wasn't about watching my team win or shivering under a blanket. It was our family time. It was at the games when we really talked, shared our secrets and confessed our sins." Chuckling, she added, "I learned how to break bad news to my parents. Wait for a base hit. And if I wanted something, like a new stereo or money for clothes, throw it out right when Will Clark was rounding third base on his way to home plate."

Devon polished off his dog, tossed the wrapper under the seat and moved close, wrapping an arm around her shoulder.

"You know," he said, "you talk a lot about your family back home."

"I do?"

"More than you think."

Nicole felt her cheeks redden. "I'm sorry. This probably bores you to death, huh?"

"On the contrary, I love hearing about it." He cleared his throat and adjusted in his seat, scooting in so he could lower his voice. "It just makes me sometimes wonder why you're here looking for people you don't even know when it seems you've got a loving family back home." She pursed her brow and he held up a hand. "I'm not judging, only asking. Help me understand this."

Another crack of the bat jerked their attention to the game, this time to see a Dodger base hit which quieted the crowd and caused Devon to slap a hand to his thigh.

"I don't know," she said. "I don't want a new family. I just want to know where I come from."

"Fair enough. But you might end up getting more than you asked for."

She looked at him inquisitively, not sure where he was going with this.

"You could end up disappointed. These people could want something you aren't able to give. Or visa versa. You say you only want to know where you come from, but are you sure you aren't looking for more? And if so, how will you feel if they can't provide it?"

She stared out over the park, Devon's words bringing a flood of emotion she hadn't expected. Had she really considered all this carefully? She thought so, but if that were true, why was she having such a hard time coming up with an answer to his question? If she truly had this matter together and her motives in check, his question should be an easy call. But instead, she only felt the need to do more thinking.

Taking a long, deep breath, she was determined to keep this conversation honest.

"Those are good points," she acknowledged. "And I've asked some of those questions, but I'll admit I don't have any good answers. I haven't sorted through all this, no."

He squeezed a hand to her shoulder. "Before you go tracking people down, I think you should."

And of course, he was right. Nicole knew that. This was all part of what had her dragging her feet these past months. Initially she'd come to Atlanta after the news of her adoption left her feeling drawn to the area. Like she was supposed to be here, as if tracking down her birth family would fill the hole in her heart and solve all the issues she now faced. But as Devon pointed out, there were things to consider, dozens of scenarios to play over in her mind, and the more she considered each one, the more reluctant she became to make a move.

It was as if her confusion created a state of its own turmoil. Things once clear were now fuzzy, and her attempts to work through it only created more fog.

"That's easier said than done," she replied.

"I don't doubt it."

He smiled in an understanding way that brought a clench to her throat. Back home, talking about this had become uncomfortable, maybe because of everyone's vested interest in the outcome. But sitting here with Devon, casually talking at the ballpark like she'd done with her family so many times before, the whole subject seemed like the natural struggles of life, not the grand upheaval she'd been embroiled in all these months. Just a problem like any other that needed to be worked out.

Devon Bradshaw was supposed to have been the distraction that took her away from her problems, not the one who reduced them all back to basics. But in a few short weeks, he'd managed to climb in close and read her more easily than she read herself. They'd fallen into a relaxed comfort with each other, his presence soothing as a hot spa.

The more time she spent with him, the more she fed on that comfort, wanting to grasp on to that security she'd lost when she'd uncovered the truth. And it was a feeling that scared the heck out of her.

Overhead, the sky darkened, making good on the earlier threat of spring showers. Before she could contemplate the last bite of her dog, she felt the first few droplets of rain.

"Welcome to Atlanta," Devon said, rising from his seat and extending a hand.

"Where are we going?"

"Considering you hate the Braves and the Dodgers, and the Dodgers are now six runs ahead, I don't think either of us see the value in sitting through a rain delay."

As the droplets grew heavier, Nicole rose from her seat and grabbed her purse. "Gotcha."

"Let's make a break for Gabe."

He grabbed her hand and they maneuvered their way through the stadium, through the crowds of people moving out of their seats and away from the rain. As Devon weaved through the sea of people, Nicole followed and watched him, for the first time feeling that weight in her chest that said this thing between them could grow into more than friendship and sex.

It was bad enough the man was sexy as sin, lighting every nerve in her body with nothing more than that one-dimpled smile. He boiled her blood in bed, dropped the tension from her shoulders and made himself that welcoming den of comfort one sought after a long day at work.

Now he'd become her analyst, sifting through nine months of garbage she'd loaded onto herself to uncover the core of why she'd come here and what she needed to do.

She'd found the kind of guy to come home to. Someone who could make sense of a world she constantly tried to confuse. He'd become the Yin to her Yang, the weight at the other end of the scale to bring balance to her life. The notion was thrilling, on one hand, frightening on the other. Because no matter how perfectly this man meshed with her needs, she wasn't convinced her needs today were the same as the long-term needs of a woman who knew who she was and where she was going.

Which should be a big fat reminder to take this all slowly.

So maybe her desire to keep Devon as a sexual distraction wasn't quite working. Maybe what was supposed to have stayed physical had somehow morphed into something more. It meant she'd have to be all that more careful to keep her emotions in check. Because if she didn't watch out, the man holding her hand could very easily take hold of her heart.

9

"DEVON, HOW COULD you do this to me?"

Devon pressed the phone closer to his ear and tried to guess the exasperated voice. "Abbey?"

"It's bad enough I had to hear it from Gavin Mitchell, but then to turn on my TV and see it broadcast on Stella Grave's segment."

It was Abbey, the only woman he knew who could carry on a conversation with herself without caring whether or not anyone knew what she was taking about. He'd called her on more than one occasion trying to tie down this date she'd won at the auction, hoping to hurry and get it out of the way. Thus, he wasn't terribly surprised to hear from her, but what she was rattling on about, he had no idea.

"Devon, when were you going to tell me you're engaged? Before or after we spent our weekend together?"

He jerked to attention and nearly dropped the phone.

"What?"

"You know, when it comes to high-end real

estate, I've got a reputation to protect. If people think I'm the other woman I could lose prospective clients."

What the hell was she talking about?

"That's what killed Renee Chadwick, you know. Word got out she was showing that billionaire more than just homes and his wife had her blackballed from the industry. She had to move to Wisconsin. Do you have any idea how cold it gets in Wisconsin?"

He held up a hand, as if that would somehow hush her through the phone.

"Abbey, what is this about an engagement?"

What is this about a weekend together? She couldn't seriously think that's what she bid on.

"You and that lottery winner. Stella told us all about it on her segment a few minutes ago."

"What did she say? And what's this about Gavin?"

"I caught up with him at Ridgewood Estates, you know, the new development he's building. When I'd mentioned our upcoming weekend at the Santiago Resort and Spa—"

Again with the weekend!

"—he said I'd better double-check that, that you've got a new love interest and you're claiming she's *the one*. Then before I can even get you on the phone, Stella Graves goes and spreads it all over Atlanta. Are you seriously engaged?"

Devon's mind was so busy trying to process everything she said, he didn't know where to start, so he picked the topic currently giving him the most distress.

"Abbey, what are you talking about, this weekend together?"

"Our weekend at the resort. I haven't forgotten and I did get your messages. I've been tied up. But now with this engagement thing—is that what you'd been calling me for? To tell me our weekend is off?"

"Abbey, there was never a weekend. It was dinner and golf."

"Devon, you don't seriously think I'd pay over three thousand dollars for just dinner and golf."

Did she actually say that?

"Yes, Abbey, it's really only dinner and golf. I'm sorry if you got the wrong impression."

"Well, it certainly doesn't matter now, does it? After what happened to Renee, I stick to available men only. Given our history, even a dinner date could look bad, particularly since your engagement has been so widely publicized."

Again with the engagement!

He opened his mouth, ready to deal with this engagement idea, when reality hit him square between the eyes.

"You're calling off the date?"

"*Hellooo,* have you heard a word I've said? It is a shame I'm out all that money, though it is a write-off for charity and I've expensed it to the realty. But if I should be audited—"

"I'll reimburse you, that's no problem," he said,

albeit a bit too eagerly. Was he truly getting out of this date with Abbey? Life would be too perfect.

"Oh, Devon, you'd do that for me?"

The tone in her voice said this was the angle she'd had in mind from the moment he picked up the phone, and it didn't bother him a bit. He'd pay twice that amount to get out of spending time with Abbey. He'd been dreading it since the auction.

"I'll have a check cut and sent to the realty this afternoon."

"You're a doll. I guess that means all the rumors I'm hearing are true." He heard her heavy sigh through the phone. "This lottery woman is one lucky gal. You will invite me to the engagement party, won't you?"

He opened his mouth to correct her, but the reality of getting the brush-off from Abbey was too much temptation. He didn't want to jinx it, so instead he smiled and said, "Absolutely!" before adding goodbyes and hanging up the phone.

How did Stella Graves get this kooky notion about an engagement? Granted, he had been somewhat vocal about his feelings for Nicole. Okay, so maybe he'd blabbed to a number of friends that he'd found *the one*. But he'd never said anything about an engagement. And even if he had, why would his love life end up on the news? Stella usually reserved her gossip for locals with more celebrity. Before now, he'd never ranked.

Leaving his office, he stopped at the desk of their Administrative Assistant, Carla Nash. Carla had worked for the firm since he was a young teen doing filing and other odd jobs for extra cash, and today she was supervising a young intern learning data entry.

"Carla," he said, taking her attention from the young man. "I need a check drafted. Let's pull it from petty cash." He grabbed the pad and pen she kept on her shelf, scribbled the details then handed her the page. "Do you think we can get that out today? I'd like Abbey to have it as soon as possible."

Carla looked at the note then back at him. "If William approves it, I don't see why not."

"Why does my dad have to approve it?"

Her dark eyes expressed confusion. "He's signing off on all payments made by the firm."

Devon frowned. "Since when?"

Carla stammered, clearly uncomfortable being put in this spot and Devon couldn't blame her. If his father had taken away his draft authority, he should have said something instead of leaving it up to her to break the news.

"Over a week ago. I thought you knew," she said. "But he's here today, so I'm sure it won't be a problem getting it signed right now."

Devon stepped down the hall, no longer concerned about getting the check out. He wanted to know what was going on. For almost a year, his father had been all but non-existent at the firm, leaving the day-to-day operations in the hands of Devon and his brothers. Now since this audit, the man had been there almost daily, insinuating himself back into the business, taking more and more control without communicating to anyone that their roles had changed.

While Bryce and Todd might be fine with it, Devon wasn't. He didn't want this job badly enough to put up with it not being his, and if his dad wanted to take it over again, the man could very well have it.

Poking his head through the opened door, Devon found his father at his desk.

"What happened to my draft authority?" he asked.

William made a face as if he'd just remembered something important he was supposed to have done. "It's only until we resolve the problems with the audit," he explained, but it was no explanation for Devon. This move was an insult, and the fact that his father had forgotten to tell him made it all that much worse.

Stepping into the office, he stood at his father's desk and crossed his arms over his chest.

"You think I'm the one siphoning money off the company? Is that what your *people* told you?"

He couldn't keep the bitterness from his tone. For two weeks now, he'd been asking his father about this *investigation,* only to be brushed off every time. This wasn't the way things were supposed to work. He was supposed to be stepping into his father's shoes, taking over this firm, and if William didn't trust him, the man should say so and relieve them both of this silly game they were apparently playing.

"Devon, the restriction applies to everyone, not you alone."

"Everyone else isn't supposed to be running this company."

The stinging look on William's face said Devon had hit his intended mark.

"Devon, I have every intention of handing over this company when the time is—"

"I don't know that I want it."

There it was. He'd finally let the words spill out, though this wasn't the time he'd planned to break the news. He'd wanted this audit resolved and things to calm down so it wouldn't seem as though his father were getting everything thrown at him at once. But the way the man had been handling things lately changed everything.

He should be mentoring Devon through the process, not keeping him out of it. And rather than go down the pointless path of explaining all this, Devon figured it was better to get on with it and let the cat out of the bag. He didn't want the business, which seemed to work out perfectly since his father apparently wasn't ready to hand it over.

The shock in his father's eyes said he hadn't expected this, which left Devon slightly surprised. He'd been dropping hints for months now. That the man hadn't paid attention spoke a few volumes of its own.

Moving back, Devon closed the door and took a seat at the desk.

"Dad, why aren't you letting me work with you on this audit? Why are you keeping the whole thing so close to the cuff?"

"I have every intention of bringing you into the process as soon as I've answered some questions."

"What questions? What is it you can't trust me with?"

"It's not a matter of trust."

"Then what is it?"

William took off his glasses and rubbed his hands over his face, and for the first time, Devon noticed how tired his father looked. Maybe this business was taking more out of the man than he expected, and if that's the case, he should be relying on his son for help.

"What do you mean you aren't sure you want the business?" William asked.

His father was intent on avoiding the topic of this audit and Devon decided to give up trying. Considering the way he felt right now, none of it mattered anyway.

"I'd like a career that's mine," he said, this particular issue providing a good back-up for his claim. "And honestly, this business of investing isn't exactly ringing my bell. For years now I've felt Bryce was the better candidate to take over this company than me."

"Bryce doesn't have your maturity."

"Bryce has what matters most—he wants it."

William rose and stepped to the window. "If you were the only son like I was, this transition would be running much more smoothly," he said, rubbing a hand over the back of his neck. "I've got all three of you to consider."

"Then let me take one of us out of the mix."

"You're not the one I want out of the mix," his father said, turning around and giving him a knowing look.

"Bryce and Todd would make a good team. They play off each other, balance each other out. They could easily run this business without me, and since you aren't in a rush to pass it over—"

"It's not that."

"—I'm just getting in the way."

William stepped back to the desk, clearly bothered by Devon's admission, which left Devon dismayed. He'd thought this might be easier. He'd thought his father would be more understanding of his need to be his own man and choose a career he really wanted, and the man's reluctance to accept what Devon was trying to tell him made this harder than he'd hoped.

"Let's get past this audit then talk about it more seriously," William offered.

Devon nearly objected, wanting to express that his mind was made up, but seeing the strain on his father's face, he didn't have the heart. Something was up. Something that was taking more out of him than he cared to admit and it burned Devon that he was being shut out like this. If it was so important to his father that he stay in the business, they should be working together to resolve the situation. But he knew his dad well enough to know that when the man decided on a path he didn't easily change direction.

His son was much the same.

"All right," he agreed. "After the audit."

Besides, he still had Nicole on his mind, and he still needed to figure out what was said during Stella's broadcast this morning.

Not that he minded the idea of he and Nicole engaged. He kind of liked thinking of her as his fiancé. He was most definitely developing feelings for the woman, feelings that felt a whole lot like love. Particularly since she'd admitted to him the circumstances around her birth, her confidence in him warmed him and demonstrated that sense of trust that he certainly wasn't getting from his family right now.

Nicole had confided in him, and he felt for her and wanted to help her through her struggles. So in that respect, maybe it was best his father was handling all this. It left him free to concentrate on what really mattered to him in his life at the moment—the woman he was growing to love.

"WEDDING PLANS?"

Nicole stared at the television in her office, still not believing what she'd seen.

"So Devon's been telling friends he's found *the one*," Penny repeated. "That's *so* romantic!"

Nicole frowned. This was not romantic at all. This was insane. They'd barely dated a month, Devon barely knew her. How could he jump to the conclusion she was *the one,* especially after confiding in him how messed up she was over her adoption? He should understand she was in no mental state for anything serious.

Eve stepped over and shut off the tape. "Clearly, someone told her you've been spotted at the bridal shops."

"For the TV show! My God, I've been to a couple porn stores for our segment on sex toys, too. What's she going to say about tha—" Nicole stopped and groaned as that thought sunk in. "Oh, I *so* don't need this."

"C'mon Nicky. We've all been in the spotlight for a while now. We should be getting used to it. Reporters are going to say what they're going to say. You've got to brush it off," Eve said.

It wasn't the reporters she was annoyed with, it was Devon. Was he really taking their relationship this seriously? Had he actually gone around town telling people he'd found the woman he was going to marry?

How could he do such a thing?

"I don't know why you're so put off by all this," Penny said. "The man's rich and gorgeous and he treats you like a queen. Now he wants to marry you? How good can life get?"

Penny's summary heightened the ache in Nicole's head. She hadn't come to Atlanta to find a husband.

She'd come here to get her head on straight, which was all the more reason why she needed to keep her love life from getting serious. She may be the new girl on the show, but she'd been around *Just Between Us* long enough to see that the worst thing a person can do is fall in love for the wrong reasons. They'd done dozens of shows on the subject and she'd interviewed countless men and women stuck in a relationship they'd ventured into because their mate had come along at a time when they were vulnerable. Years later, they wake up and realize everything about their life has gone wrong, but now they're stuck with children to consider, people they could destroy and the passing years working against them. All because of one wrong move at one right time.

"I'm not marrying anyone," Nicole insisted, moving back to her desk.

"It's highly possible Stella Graves warped Devon's words the same way she warped your visits to bridal stores. She got you wrong, she probably got him wrong, too," Eve assured.

Nicole's intercom buzzed, and she pressed the button for the line.

"Nicole, Devon Bradshaw's here to see you."

She eyed Eve and Penny with a look that said she'd soon find out.

"Let him through, thanks. He knows the way to my office."

Eve ushered Penny out and before she followed,

paused briefly to add, "Be nice. Ask questions. Don't draw assumptions."

Nicole simply frowned then began pacing her office until she heard the voice behind her.

"Hey, beautiful."

She turned on her heels, her arms folded tightly across her chest. "We need to talk."

He quirked a brow. "Let me guess—Stella Graves."

"So you saw it."

Stepping into the office, he closed the door behind him. "No, but I heard. That's why I'm here. I figured it being a TV station someone might have taped it."

Nicole stepped over to the television, rewound the tape and after pressing a couple buttons, the black screen filled with Stella Graves' eager smile. Next to her were photos of both Nicole and Devon, displayed on screen as if they were the latest hot item since Bennifer and Brangelina. Nicole recognized her photo as one taken when she and the group were introduced at a press conference as winners of Lot'O'Bucks.

In the brief segment, Stella speculated that the budding relationship—which started with the bachelor auction three weeks ago—had turned serious and that these two wealthy socialites might be heading for a merger.

"Socialites?" Devon repeated, obviously surprised they'd been propelled up to the ranks of Atlanta's elite.

But Nicole could care less about that. For over a

month, all the members of the lottery group had been the subject of headlines. She'd become used to it. It was Devon's proclamations of something serious that struck the tightest nerve. According to Stella, he hadn't been shy about telling friends and family marriage was in his future, and when Stella quoted him in the segment, Nicole pointed to the screen.

"I'm *the one?*"

Devon shrugged. "I might have said something along those lines to one or two friends."

"How could you?"

He held up his hands. "Whoa, now wait a minute. *You're* the one trying on bridal gowns. I simply said you were marriage material."

"Marriage material?"

"What's wrong with that?"

"Well, for one thing, it's on the news!"

He casually rubbed his chin. "Yeah, my guess is Tom Watts. He's a golfing buddy and his wife's got a big mouth. She happens to know Stella, too."

"How could you tell your golfing buddies we're getting married?!"

Picking up on her distress, he crossed his arms over his chest in defense. "I didn't tell my golfing buddies we're getting married. I mean, not in the sense that we're getting married *now*. I can only guess *that* little stretch came from your recent bridal shopping spree."

She clamped her hands to her hips, her heart

beating faster with every word he uttered. "I didn't go on a bridal shopping spree! I mean—I did—but not for me. It's for the show. That's what *I do,* you know."

"And, there you have it. She took a stupid off-handed comment by me and put it together with your job and made up a story. Mystery solved."

"How can you be so casual about this?"

"Why are *you* making such a big deal out of it? She's a silly gossip reporter. Everyone knows she makes up half of what she says."

"I can't believe you could go around town blabbing to people about our relationship."

Devon frowned. "Well excuse me. I'm not used to being involved with a celebrity." Pointing a finger, he added, "*You're* the one they're interested in here."

She dropped her jaw. "Are you saying this is all my fault?"

"Hell, we certainly aren't on the news because of me."

"Ha!" she squeaked. "This can't be happening."

As she stood there agape, Devon moved next to her and slipped a hand around her waist.

"Hon, look, I'm just asking you to cut me some slack. I'm not used to being in the spotlight. I said a couple wrong things to the wrong people. It won't happen again." Pulling her close, he bent and murmured into her ear. "And if you stop by my place tonight, I'd be happy to make it up to you."

He palmed her ass and pressed his waist against

hers in a move that turned him hard and her mushy all in one shot. His lips went to work on the tender skin below her ear, his warm breath heated her blood, he brushed a thumb against her nipple and clasped her breast, all of it working together to send a whirlpool of sensation straight to places it shouldn't.

Damn, the man had moves. She was supposed to be angry. They were in her office, no less! But in one swift motion, he'd managed to erase her thoughts and numb her brain to the point where, if pressed, she couldn't recall a word of what they'd been talking about.

"I've missed you," he whispered under her chin. "It's been two whole days since I've been inside you."

She gulped and wrapped an arm around his waist to stay focused, and when he slid a hand between her thighs, her sex pulsed in response.

"You're naughty," she said through a sigh. "We're in my office."

"And oh, what I'd love to do with you splayed across your desk."

He bent and pressed his erection against her most sensitive spot, and she actually wondered if they'd be able to pull off sex in her office...during business hours...given the lock on her door didn't work.

"You're a bad, bad boy," she said.

His light chuckle feathered against her neck and she rolled her head back, her muscles no longer able to support the weight.

"Do you think we could do it here?" she whispered.

"With you, I could do it anywhere."

"Someone might come."

"I certainly hope we both do."

She smiled and giggled over the joke, and be damned if she wasn't actually considering tossing off her slacks right there in the station.

Until she heard a light rap on the door.

"Nicole?"

They both jumped and straightened, and while they ran a quick clothing check, Nicole shakily called out, "Just a minute."

She found herself in order, but unfortunately Devon's loose wool pants did nothing to restrain one very stiff cock.

"Make that two minutes," he said softly, moving around and taking a quick seat behind her desk.

Penny called through the door, "I just wanted to tell you your eleven o'clock appointment is here."

Damn. She forgot all about her meeting…and her job…and what the heck Devon had come here for in the first place. It was all a low buzz, but in her confusion she managed to say, "I'll be right there."

Devon handed her a folder that had the meeting time posted on a bright green sticky note attached. "Do you need this?"

"Thanks," she said, brushing a hand down her blouse and then smoothing her slacks.

"My place? Tonight?" he asked.

"Oh, yeah."

10

"How does Chinese sound?"

"Like the perfect after-sex meal," Nicole said. Stretched out next to Devon, she rested her head on his shoulder while she toyed with the hairs on his chest, a tossing of blankets spread loosely over them. "You've left me with an appetite."

He caressed a hand over her shoulder. "Well, after seeing you in your office this morning, I could never quite shake the tent from my pants. It made for a rather uncomfortable afternoon."

She lifted the blanket, glanced between his legs and teased, "We fixed that."

"Momentarily."

At least they fixed one thing, she thought, though they still had the issue of Stella's segment to discuss. Nicole knew Devon probably considered the matter closed, but all afternoon she'd been bothered by the things he'd said to his friends, this idea she was marriage material, their relationship getting serious. On more than one occasion, she'd seen the signs and had even felt that certain tug herself, which was all the more reason they needed to clear the air about where this relationship was going. Or *not* going, to be more precise.

"So, Devon," she started, pausing to make sure she formed the right words. "This whole thing about me being *the one*...that's mere talk, right? I mean, you aren't really serious about that."

He quirked a brow. "Would it bother you if I was?"

The relaxation their lovemaking had provided gave way to sudden tension. "In a sense, yes. I'm not in the right frame of mind for anything serious."

She lifted off his shoulder and propped up on one elbow to get a better view of his expression and succumbing to her sudden need to put some physical distance between them.

"Because of the adoption," he said.

"I thought you understood."

He sat up, his face clearly stating he didn't. "I understand you're struggling right now, I just don't get what that has to do with us." Scooting up farther, he leaned against the headboard, apparently readying himself for the conversation Nicole now realized they should have had before this.

"Nicole, you're confused, and I don't blame you for it. I would be, too."

"Then you see why this whole thing between us needs to stay casual."

Instead of answering, he sat and stared, prompting her to slip off the bed and gather her clothes.

"Devon," she said, pulling on her slacks and

reaching for her bra. "I didn't come here to fall in love and get engaged, I came here to figure out who I am."

"So why haven't you done that?"

"Because I haven't had time."

"What have you done to find your birth parents?"

"I told you, I haven't had time."

"I think you have, you're just choosing not to."

Her annoyance brimmed and she moved more quickly to pull on her clothes and get dressed. "You're changing the subject. This is about us, not my adoption."

Rolling out of bed, Devon grabbed a pair of sweats off a chair and pulled them on. "No, this is about us *and* your adoption. I'm not stupid, Nicole. It's that I disagree."

"Disagree with what?"

"This notion you've got to figure this out on your own." He stood and stared as she slipped her top over her head. "There's nothing to figure out," he said. "This adoption didn't change who you are and I think you know that. You're only angry because your family lied to you. In an unconscious way, you want to punish them so you moved away under the guise of finding your birth parents. But your own spite leaves you uncomfortable. You don't want to be angry so you've convinced yourself you're here to sort things out. Problem is that's not really what you want and now that you've done all this you're sitting here in limbo trying to plan your next move."

She scoffed. "What are you, a psychiatrist?"

"No. I'm the first objective person you've confided in and I can read you like a book. It's one of the many reasons I'm certain we belong together. You've got no choice but to be real with me."

She stepped across the room and slipped into her shoes, absently searching the room for any clothing items she might have missed while she tried to collect her thoughts. This wasn't at all what she'd expected. She'd planned to simply clear the air and come to an agreement that this thing between them needed to stay casual.

She hadn't expected a psych session or professions that they were fated to be together.

"I am being real, and right now, I really need my space," she insisted.

"If you needed your space, you wouldn't be showing up at my place every other night after work."

"That's not fair."

"No, what's not fair is that you aren't considering anything I'm saying." He moved up behind her and placed his hands on her shoulders and her body both cringed and relaxed all in one mixture of confusion. "You know exactly who you are. This adoption didn't change that, and neither has moving to Atlanta. You're the funny, beautiful, smart woman I'm falling in love with."

The comment dropped her throat to her stomach and she turned around, still in his arms.

"In love with?"

"Nicole, I'm crazy about you. And I know you're confused and hurt but I also know that together we can get past this."

She wriggled out from under him and stepped away, shaking her head as she tried to absorb his words. "Love is way too big a word for what we have."

"Not when it comes to my feelings for you."

A headache began brewing between her temples. This conversation was barreling in the wrong direction with the force of a high-speed train and she needed to stop it.

"I know what you need, Nicole. You need to stop trying to deal with this on your own."

"I had plenty of help back in California."

"With family too close to the situation and too invested in how you felt about all this." He crossed his arms over his chest. "Admit you're angry with them."

"I'm angry with everything, including this conversation." Pressing her fingers to the bridge of her nose, she added, "If you know me so well, you'll understand why I can't even consider getting involved with you or anyone else right now."

"Why?"

"Because I'm too vulnerable, that's why."

"You aren't the least bit vulnerable. You're the strongest woman I know. You're just confused, there's a big difference."

"Fine, I'm confused, and having you talk about love isn't helping."

He bowed his head and sighed. "You're right. I'm sorry. I hadn't expected to have this conversation today and I take full responsibility for the rumors Stella started this morning." Meeting her gaze, he added, "But it doesn't change my feelings. We have something special that I think we should explore."

"What I need to explore is myself, not us."

"And I can help you, if you'd let me."

These were the same words she'd heard from her parents, her friends and her brother. They'd all gathered around and smothered her with their good intentions, trying to tell her how she should feel, what kind of opinion she should have and how to go on with her life. But not one of them could put themselves in her shoes any more than Devon could right now.

"I don't need help, I need distance. I need everyone to stop telling me who I'm supposed to be and how I'm supposed to feel, and instead, leave me alone."

She didn't mean to snap off so sharply, and the moment the words came out of her mouth she regretted the tone. But she didn't regret the content. Devon was right. She'd been using him as another distraction, showing up at his apartment after work because going home left her alone with her thoughts. And though being alone with her thoughts was uncomfortable, it was time for her to suck it up and deal with it the way she'd wanted. The way she'd intended.

"You need to let the people who care about you help."

"The people who care about me only want to protect what they want. My parents don't want to lose their daughter, my brother doesn't want to lose his sister, my friends don't want to lose the Nicole they've always known."

"Do you want to lose them?"

"They were never mine to keep."

"That's the spite talking. I don't think that's how you feel."

She looked into his eyes, her own welling with tears. "That's the problem. I don't know how I feel. And until I sort this out on my own, I'll never truly trust that my feelings are my own and not someone else's."

He shook his head and spoke softly. "Nicole, this is so much simpler than you're making it."

Darting out of the bedroom, she moved to the front entryway and reached for her sweater and purse then turned to face him as he followed. "I'm sorry, Devon. What I need is to stop dragging my feet and deal with things like I'd planned. I need to back off from this relationship," she said, her throat closing with every word. "Maybe once I get past this, if you're still interested in spending time with me, we can come back around and do this thing right."

"We aren't doing it wrong."

"Yes, we are. I'm not ready for this." Turning,

she opened the door and offered the only thing she could as she walked away for good.

"I'm sorry."

"I PUSHED TOO HARD too soon," Devon said, drowning his anger in a beer. Next to him, his sister, Grace, sipped on a marguerita. He didn't usually stop in bars after work, nor ask his sister to join him, but since the break-up with Nicole last night, he needed a beer and a woman's opinion.

"Of course, you did. It's what you do."

He frowned. "You know, some people complain that I move too slowly."

"Not when you decide you want something. Then it's full speed ahead and be damned with everyone else."

His frown deepened. That wasn't true at all. Case in point being the fact that he'd decided he wanted out of the family business but he was still hanging on. He had the patience to wait until the timing was right.

Okay, so maybe he blurted his intentions to his father sooner than he'd planned, but— "I brought you here for advice, not a free personality analysis."

"And that's what I'm giving you. She told you she needs time, that she needs to sort through her problems on her own, and you asked me what to do. I'm saying—here's a thought—how about doing what she asked?"

Grace crossed her long legs and sipped her drink, those blue eyes filled with a smirky sisterly arrogance.

"Because she needs me. I'm telling you, she's making this whole adoption issue way bigger than it needs to be."

"Really? I didn't know you were an expert on adoption."

"I'm not. I'm an expert on Nicole."

"In three weeks?"

"Four."

"Well," Grace huffed. "You must be in some sort of expedited learning program. Brad and I have been married three years and he still hasn't figured me out."

"No one ever will," Devon teased, prompting Grace to elbow him.

She sighed and smiled warmly. "Seriously, Devon, I like Nicole. I like her a lot. And heaven knows I'd love to have another woman in the family. I believe you probably could help her, but the bottom line is she's not ready to accept your help. Until she's ready to listen, there's nothing you can do." She patted his thigh. "You want to give the answers to her and it's just not going to work that way."

He drained his beer glass then eyed the bartender and motioned for another. "It's frustrating dealing with Nicole when this is all so simple."

"Maybe it's *not* simple. How do you know?"

"Remember Leeanne, the woman I dated a couple years ago? You liked her. I liked her. She and I got along great and when we broke up, you asked me what went wrong."

"I remember."

"I told you nothing went wrong per se, but that she wasn't *the one*."

"So what does that have to do with Nicole being simple?"

"Because Nicole *is* the one. I knew it the moment I saw her. And I knew *her* the moment I saw her. I couldn't explain what went wrong when it came to Leeanne, and I can't explain what's right about Nicole. It's just that feeling. And as much as I feel I know her, I know I can help her." Clinking his beer to her glass, he added, "And you're supposed to be telling me how to do that."

Grace took on a look of concentration and he hoped that meant she was going to give him an answer he could work with. Nicole had been stagnating here in Atlanta for nine months not making any progress. Another nine months probably wouldn't change things.

Grace sighed sympathetically. "I don't know, Devon. I wish I knew what else to say. Maybe give her a week or two to absorb what you'd already said then see her again. I just keep thinking the quiet persuasion is better than full frontal force."

It was the last thing he cared to do, but he doubted he had a choice. Grace was right. He'd played too many cards too fast and now he was stuck trying to backtrack.

"In the meantime," she said, "you can tell me about you leaving the firm."

"That didn't take any time at all," he grumbled.

Was there nothing private in this family?

"Mom's worried. She says dad's been stressed for weeks but she's evasive when I ask why. Then yesterday, she tells me you want to quit the firm."

"I haven't officially quit the firm. I said I wasn't sure it was the job or the future I wanted."

Grace smiled. "You wouldn't have said that if you hadn't already opted out."

"No, I suppose not."

"What the hell's going on?"

He sucked in a breath and sighed. "There's the question of the week. All I know is we had some discrepancies with our annual audit, Dad's all but taken his old job back and he's not saying a thing to any of us."

He pulled a dish of mixed nuts toward them and tossed one in his mouth. "Dad pulled our draft authority at the office. He's the only one in the company who can approve checks. Personally, that pissed me off, but when I asked Bryce and Todd what they thought about it, they shrugged it off." He shook his head and added, "Something's not right with that."

"I wouldn't read much into that. The rest of us are already accustomed to living on the sidelines. You're only now getting a taste of what life's like when you're not the Golden Child."

"I'm hardly the Golden Child. And besides, that's rather ironic coming from the family princess."

"Speaking of which, are you going to take me

home in your carriage so I can finish this margue-rita? It's going to my head."

"Drink up," he said.

"I'm serious about giving Nicole some space."

"I heard you."

"Yeah, and I also know how much you like fol-lowing my advice when it contradicts what you want to do."

"That's only when it comes to your unsolicited advice. This time I asked, remember?"

"Yeah, and I can already see the wheels turning in your head. I told you to back off, but you aren't going to do that, are you?"

"I'm taking all your advice to heart."

"And then tomorrow, you'll do exactly what *you* want."

Instead of answering, he simply raised his glass in a toast. "To all the women in my life who know me but love me anyway."

Grace raised a brow. "That would be me and mom."

He smiled and tapped his glass to hers. "I've got to start somewhere."

_11_

DEVON STRODE DOWN THE hall of CATL-TV on his way to Nicole's office. He'd done as Grace suggested, giving Nicole some time—if three days counted—then decided to see if she'd accept an impromptu lunch. He'd considered calling, but decided he'd rather offer the invite in person. If she said no, he wanted to at least read the expression on her face and feel the vibes in the room to better determine his options.

Because despite the way she'd left things, he still believed he had options.

So he'd made one crap move admitting he was falling for her. It was hardly reversible. But he could slow things down to whatever pace she needed. And when it came to her issues about her adoption, well, she was right, he wasn't a psychiatrist. Who was he to say what was simple and what wasn't?

All he knew was that she didn't have to go through it alone. He could help her if she'd let him.

Waiting in the lobby, Penny came through the door to escort him in. In her arms was a large plastic bag filled with lime green feathers. He didn't ask.

He'd dropped by the station enough times to realize on a show like this, you never knew what you'd see in the halls and it was typically best not to pry. The explanations he got were sometimes scary.

"Is Nicole here?" he asked.

Penny nodded. "She's interviewing a couple who've been married and divorced four times—to each other."

"That's taking on-again-off-again to the extreme."

"Tell me about it." She looked at her watch. "I don't think she'll be much longer, though. If you want, you can wait in her office. I can slip her a note and let her know you're here."

"I'll wait, but don't bother with the note. I'd rather surprise her."

He followed her through the station and took a seat in one of the chairs at Nicole's desk then pulled his cell from his suit jacket to check the time on tonight's Braves game. As he flipped open the phone something on Nicole's desk caught his eye. A dark brown folder had his name on it, and he wondered if it had to do with the show on charity bachelor auctions. Though he'd discussed it with Nicole on more than one occasion, he hadn't expected to be part of the segment. They'd booked a number of other men who did the auctions on a more regular basis, so Devon had opted out.

Picking up the folder, he opened it and what he saw threw him completely. It wasn't notes on bachelor auctions but what looked like a background check.

Pages and pages of details including his address history, a criminal check detailing the speeding ticket he'd gotten last summer, a listing of possible relatives, a property report—it went on and on.

What the hell was this?

He tried to wrap his mind around why Nicole would have pulled together so much information on him. Was she worried he may be keeping something from her?

And if she had, what did he think of that?

Before he had a chance to go down that road, his thoughts were sideswiped by his credit report. Included with his credit cards were personal loans totaling upwards of three hundred thousand dollars, none of which he'd applied for. His first thought was identity theft. The credit had been approved several weeks ago and money had been distributed on one of the loans. Payments had been made, which meant statements must have been sent, but where?

Then something else hit him, causing him to turn back to the address history he'd glanced at before.

His eyes scanned the page a second time until he found it. His name was listed under Todd's downtown apartment. Why would his name be listed at Todd's address? He and Todd never shared a place, not since living at home with their parents.

He tried to think of a rational explanation but too many questions were coming at him at once. Why did Nicole have this on her desk? How could loans this large have been granted under his name without his knowledge? And then the most sinking feeling of all—was Todd behind this?

Bits and pieces of information came flooding back to him. The audit at work. Suspicious payments wreaking havoc with everyone at the firm—except Todd. There'd been a number of occasions when Todd had been questioned, and he'd brushed them off every time. Everyone had been expressing concern, but Todd continually said it was nothing. Except it wasn't nothing. They all saw what this mess was doing to their father. It had been aging the man. He'd been riddled with concern. It's what frustrated Devon the most; that his father wouldn't let him help, wouldn't let him shoulder some of the burden.

Devon hadn't understood, but if Todd were behind this it would all make sense. Even his father's subtle comments on why he was being so evasive about the audit.

He looked back over the dates when these loans were made and noticed they coincided with when questions had started being raised about the missing money at work. These two situations had to be linked.

Which meant his brother was pulling something foul and their father probably knew about it. No other scenario seemed plausible. In fact, this was the only thing that made all the events of the last couple of months fit with one another.

But what was it exactly?

His head spinning with questions, he rose from

the chair and backed away from the desk. Several people had some explaining to do, starting with Todd, but as he moved to leave the office, Nicole met him at the door.

"Devon," she said, her eyes wide with surprise.

He stopped in his tracks, still clutching the folder in his hands. "What is this?" he asked.

She glanced at the file then back to him. "It's a background check. I'm researching a segment."

"A segment on *what?*"

Her brow furrowed when she realized he was distressed. "It's a segment about knowing who you're getting involved with."

"By running their credit history?"

Glancing behind her, she stepped into her office and closed the door. "That and a number of other services offered to prospective couples."

"Prospective couples?"

She moved to her desk and set down the file she'd been holding. "Devon, this isn't personal. I haven't even looked at the information. I'd been interviewing a man who offered these services for people who want to check up on who they're sleeping with. He'd offered it as part of the interview. I hadn't even thought twice about it."

"Do you?"

"Do I what?"

"Want to check up on your lover."

She made a face he didn't like, the kind of face that said he had no right to be put off by any of this.

"This isn't about us. This is about truth. And yes, I do think people have a right to know who they're getting involved with. Why would anyone object unless they had something to hide?"

Something to hide? Wasn't that one big mountain of irony? Someone was obviously trying to scam him, and how did he find that out? Because his girlfriend ran a background check on him.

How was he supposed to turn all this into something rational?

"I don't know why you're making such a big deal out of it," she said. "These are just samples of services available to couples." Shuffling through the files on her desk, she brought out another folder. "I ordered one on me, too. I haven't opened either of them."

He snorted. "Well, you might want to take a look. You never know what people have been doing behind your back."

"That's exactly the point. I'd think you'd understand why I might have a personal bias on this issue. Don't you think people have the right to the truth?"

Devon didn't know what he thought. He was still too busy trying to sort out the things he'd found, trying to place some logical explanation around it in a way that didn't involve being betrayed by his brother, lied to by his father and investigated by his girlfriend. All he knew was that his life had just gotten complicated, and maybe this was Fate's way of showing him that Nicole had been correct all along. Maybe he had moved too far too fast, pushing her to a level of intimacy she wasn't ready for. If this was the kind of thing she needed in order to feel secure with him, maybe her problems went deeper than he could handle.

He tossed the file on her desk. "Here you go. Have all the truth you want."

She huffed. "Why do you look so angry? It's a simple background check."

"Because I happen to believe in such a thing as trust." He pointed a finger to the file. "So your folks lied to you. I won't dismiss that. But is this the life they've left you with? Background checks and private eyes? You got screwed once so you'll never trust the human race again?"

She opened her mouth then shut it, apparently sidetracked by the question, and when she did speak, the tone lacked her prior resolve.

"Not everyone tells the truth."

"No, I suppose they don't," he said, recalling the information in his file and the questions churning his thoughts. "And worse, when we do uncover the truth, we don't always like what we find."

NICOLE STARED AT THE doorway as Devon walked out, still in a daze over what had happened. Sure, not everyone agreed with the idea of background checks. That was part of the controversy of their upcoming show. But she'd thought Devon, of all people, would recognize her side of it.

For a brief moment, she fought the urge to catch up with him, but decided it was best to let him go. More than once over the last few days she'd caught herself wondering whether or not he'd call. He'd said he was falling in love with her, a sentiment that scared her witless. And worse, though she wasn't anywhere near ready for love and marriage, she had to admit to a sense of loss she'd been trying to deny.

She stared at the doorway wondering for a second time if she should chase him down, but what message would that send? She'd told him she needed to back off and she'd meant it. They obviously didn't see eye-to-eye when it came to issues of trust, and his anger about the file confirmed it. If he loved her as he'd said, he would have been more understanding.

Right?

Moving to her desk, she plopped down and sighed, not totally sure of anything. She didn't know what he saw in that file of his, but her gut told her he'd been angry about more than that. Was there something in there he hadn't expected? And if so, was it really any of her business to find out for herself?

"How did your interview go?"

She looked up to see Eve standing in her doorway and she put on a casual smile. "Taping over already?"

"Fridays are easy, remember? We don't have a lot of prep work for audience participation day." Eve stepped into the office and took a seat.

"That's right," Nicole said. She picked up the file associated with the meeting she'd just had. "Craig and Donna Wells are a bust. In fact, that whole segment idea on couples reuniting probably isn't going to work. At least not with the people we slated for the show."

"That bad, huh?"

"Nothing romantic about this couple's four weddings. Basically, they're two crazies who've turned breaking up into an art form." Pulling her notes from the pad and tucking them into the folder, she admitted they weren't a story as much as they were simply two people who couldn't make up their minds about what they wanted from life. Nicole had been hoping for something more romantic, maybe two soul mates that the world kept tearing apart, but that wasn't the case. They were just a couple who refused to resolve their problems. When things got tough, they found it easier to hit divorce court than attack the real issues.

Funny, how easily she could analyze everyone but herself.

"So if they're bust what else have we got?" Eve asked.

Stuffing the folder in her file cabinet, Nicole moved to the pair of background checks that had been delivered that morning.

"I've got what the P.I did for *Rate Your Mate Before It's Too Late.*"

Eve's eyes brightened. "The background research you ordered on you and Devon?"

Nicole nodded but didn't share Eve's excitement. Instead, she tried to brush off her visit from Devon and the nagging feeling it left in her gut.

"So anything juicy in them?"

"I haven't looked," she said.

Eve stared at her with surprise. "Why not?"

"I'm just not sure this is any of our business."

"I don't get it, what's with the big change of pace? Last time we talked, you were set on the idea people had a right to know what their lover might not be telling them."

And up until a moment ago, Nicole wouldn't have thought twice about looking through Devon's file. But now she wasn't so sure.

Because I happen to believe in such a thing as trust.

Devon's words came back to her, boring a hole in the new attitude she'd formed during the last year. She'd believed in trust too, once, and in her hurt and anger she'd shoved it aside thinking trust was for fools.

But who was the fool, really?

Too many times lately suspicion and doubt had stopped her from getting what she wanted. It had paralyzed her and left her motionless when she should have moved forward. Though she felt people had a right to the truth, she didn't know if this method was the answer. In fact, the longer she con-

sidered it, the less confident she felt about everything, and Devon's words hadn't helped.

Was it true? Was she so damaged that her future
was relegated to background checks and investiga-
tions in order to trust in the people she loved?

"Oh, I don't know," she said with a sigh, more
confused now than she'd been ten minutes ago.
"When I started this segment, it had all seemed
simple. There was truth and there were lies. But the
farther I get into it, the more I'm realizing the impor-
tance of faith." She eyed Eve. "Where does that fit in?"

"It's a point I think we should explore, for sure."

Nicole grabbed both files and shoved them in her
desk. "I'm thinking the whole angle of the show
needs to be reworked." Pushing up from her chair
she began pacing her office. "That woman, Nancy
Shepard, the one who got scammed for thirty
thousand dollars, do you think background checks
are the answer to her problems?"

"No, what she could use is her thirty grand
back."

Nicole frowned. "I'm serious. This segment has
been completely focused on people protecting
themselves from getting burned, particularly people
who've been there before, but the more I think
about it, the more I just don't know anymore."

"What else is there?"

"Healing."

"Healing?" Eve asked.

"Files like this," she said, gesturing toward the

drawer. "Do they solve problems or avoid them? Maybe instead of reacting to betrayal by not trusting the people we meet, we should be trying to heal the pain instead."

"There's nothing wrong with that." Eve tapped a finger to her lips. "In fact, I like that a lot. It's way more positive. It digs into the deeper issues."

"The problem is how do you heal?"

Eve shrugged. "Why don't we call Dr. Lennox?"

Dr. Lennox was a therapist they brought onto the show when they felt the need for an expert opinion, but Nicole wasn't satisfied with getting a therapist's opinion and leaving it at that. She'd seen two of them back in California and neither had gone far in the way of helping her sort out her problems. At the time, they'd simply become another voice in her ear telling her how she was supposed to feel or that the feelings she had were normal.

That wasn't what she'd wanted to hear. That she had a right to be mad and confused didn't help her figure out how to move on with her life. It just kept her mad and confused.

Though she wasn't opposed to Dr. Lennox, she wanted more.

"I'm thinking of that woman," she said, moving back to her desk and pulling out the file. "Sylvia Grey. Her husband had been married to another woman for the entire ten years of their marriage and she never knew about it. They even had a child. Yet three years after putting him in jail for bigamy, she remarried."

"What did she have to say about it?"

Nicole glanced over the notes, rereading the interview. Sylvia was one of the first women she'd met with and Nicole remembered being skeptical, but she couldn't remember why. Scanning the notes, she came upon the issue. "I'd asked her how she learned to trust again and she said you just do it. That there isn't a choice."

Nicole remembered thinking that was too simplistic, that the audience wouldn't accept that. She knew *she* hadn't.

Moving farther down the page, she saw another note she'd forgotten. "She said it was about finding the right people to support her and accepting their help. She said there wasn't a miracle cure. It simply took time and patience and understanding."

Lowering to her chair, Nicole let the comment hang in the air between them. She remembered Sylvia more clearly, reading over those notes. She hadn't wanted to hear what the woman had to say. It had sounded passive, like a time heals all wounds cliché. And she'd dismissed the new husband's part in it all, how much his patience and understanding helped Sylvia get through her problems. And though Nicole still wasn't sure this would make a good show, she was feeling better about this angle than the idea of hiring private eyes to check out lovers.

Now that she thought about it, that wasn't the answer at all. Devon was right—that type of thinking only furthered the paranoia, adding fuel to the notion that people couldn't be trusted, and avoiding the issue of healing altogether.

"This needs to be a show about renewing faith, not protecting ourselves against creeps."

"Why am I getting the impression we're talking about more than the show?"

Nicole shrugged. "I've been there, you know that. And I'm beginning to think a good offense isn't always the best defense." Shuffling the pages back in order, she placed them in the folder. "So we've got a new angle with the segment?"

Eve nodded. "I like it. Like I said, it's more positive. Let's go with it." She gave Nicole the thumbs up and left her office. Nicole pulled open the desk drawer with the background checks, this time with the intent of taking them both to the shredder. But before she did, she went ahead and opened hers, looking through the information and seeing nothing untoward. There were the parking tickets she'd accumulated when her friend Reyna moved to the house on Geary. That was a pain in the ass, and though she missed Reyna, she didn't miss the old parking situation.

Nicole's credit score was better than she'd expected, bringing a smile to her face. Several pages had her birth date, but didn't reference her adoption, and as she thumbed through the papers, she was pleased to see no other surprises to greet her.

It was a good thing. One shock in a lifetime was enough, thank you.

Closing the file she glanced at Devon's and wondered what he'd seen. He'd been angry she'd ordered this file, and when all was said and done, she couldn't really blame him. That hadn't been the right approach to dealing with her problems, and she intended to take a new direction starting now.

Picking up Devon's file, she carried it to the shredder, shoving the pages through without glancing at a solitary tidbit. It was time to move forward and explore all those issues she and Devon had discussed when they'd talked at the ballpark. She would weigh the pros and cons of searching down her birth parents, and even if she had to chart out every scenario on a big white board, that's what she'd do. But one thing was for sure, living another day in limbo would no longer be an option.

12

"EXPLAIN THIS." Devon slapped the loan papers on Todd's desk and waited for a reaction. On his way back from the station, he'd made a few stops gathering up paperwork on these accounts that had shown up under his name. The effort had confirmed his suspicions; his little brother had been falsifying loan applications and walking away with tens of thousands in Devon's name.

And he wanted to know why.

The look on Todd's face said he wasn't prepared for this, which only fueled Devon's anger. Did Todd actually think he'd never get caught? Had he assumed Devon was so witless he wouldn't notice credit of this magnitude being issued under his name?

"Oh, man, I was going to tell you about that."

"Yeah? And what were you going to say?"

"Look, I'd just tapped out all my resources and didn't have anywhere else to go."

"You couldn't have asked me for the money?"

Todd's trapped expression turned to surprise. "Would you have given it to me?"

"You never gave me that option, did you?" He

stepped away from the desk and began pacing the office, feeling the need to put some distance between him and his brother before he succumbed to the impulse to grab the man by the throat and shake out why he'd done this.

"How could you have tapped out all your resources?" Devon asked. "What kind of financial shape are you in?"

"I'm flat broke. I can't get any more credit and I can't borrow from any more friends. I would have asked but I couldn't afford for you to turn me down."

Devon stopped pacing and stared at Todd. How could the man possibly be broke? They all made hefty salaries as executives of the firm, in addition to commission on the investments. Nobody in the family was hurting.

"What the hell do you spend your money on?"

Todd held up his hands and shrugged. "Things got a little out of hand. I swung a couple of bad deals, made one or two bad bets and it snowballed."

"You went broke *gambling?*"

Todd scoffed. "You know, you're just as hypocritical as Dad. Our whole business of investing is nothing more than gambling with people's money. You lose here and it's simply a bad return. I lose in Vegas and I'm suddenly some kind of idiot."

Devon stood for a moment, trying to grasp the situation. "Exactly how much did you lose?"

"It doesn't matter. Dad's getting it under control."

"So dad *is* in on this."

"We're putting all the money back. Once we fix the audit and get Bryce squared away—"

"*Bryce* knows about this, too?"

Todd looked at him as though that should have been obvious. "He hadn't been until recently. But he is in charge of the audit. We didn't have a choice." Shaking his head, he added, "I never would have cut into the firm. I know better than that, but they were going to kill me."

"What?" Devon stepped to the conference table and dropped into one of the chairs. "How could you get yourself into such a mess and then drag Dad and Bryce into it?"

"What was I supposed to do? I'd run out of answers. I'd tried taking out loans to pay back the company but it was too late. By then, the auditors had already clamped down on the books."

Devon lowered his face to his hands and sat for a moment.

Todd had always been a gambler. Heck, their mother used to get him to eat his peas as a kid by betting him a dollar he couldn't do it. The man flew to Vegas several times a year, spent his weekends at the track, and none of it had seemed like a cause for concern up until now. But this kind of debt, this kind of a mess was most definitely causing concern.

"Oh, hell," Devon said with a sigh. "How much are you in for?"

"Nothing, now. The bookies are all paid off. We only need to cover what I borrowed from the firm."

"Borrowed?"

"I'm paying every cent back. I'd just had a bad streak is all, but my luck is turning."

Devon looked up at his brother, aghast. "You can't still be gambling."

"I told you, things got out of hand, but I've got everything under control."

"No, what you've got is a gambling problem."

Todd smirked. "Everyone gambles. But I know my limits now. And Dad's squaring away the audit." Frowning, he added, "You're worrying too much about this."

Devon couldn't believe his ears. His brother had nearly gotten killed, had jeopardized the family business, yet spoke as if everything was perfectly in order.

"If you even think you can keep gambling, you need professional help."

"I'm all right."

"No. You're not," he said.

"Look, I told you I was sorry. We're putting the money back. What more do you want from me?"

Shaking his head, Devon grabbed the paperwork and turned toward the door. "More than you're willing to deal with," he said, before storming out. He made his way down the hall to his father's office, needing to get a sane perspective on this mess.

"You okay, son?" William asked, hanging up a call as Devon walked in.

Devon pushed the documents in front of his father. "Why didn't you tell me about Todd?"

William scanned the top page and looked away. "I'm taking care of that. Those accounts will be closed—"

"I already closed them and paid off the debt."

"You didn't have to do that."

"Neither did you, but considering what this cost me, I think I deserve to know what's been happening."

William rubbed a hand over his face and Devon noticed again how tired his father seemed. He had bags under his eyes, his skin was blotched and ashen. His cheeks appeared drawn, as if he'd been doing more drinking than eating lately, and Devon cursed his brother for putting this kind of stress on the man.

"Todd got himself into trouble," his father said.

"Todd's got a gambling problem."

"That he does."

"I don't understand why you didn't confide in me. I'm supposed to be taking over this company." Holding up the papers, he added, "These are my personal finances. Why didn't you bring me in on this?"

"It's Todd's matter."

"No, it's a family matter, one we should be handling together."

William sighed and nodded consent. "I suppose you're right. Although, this has to be kept close to the vest and I figured the fewer people who knew about it the better."

Lowering to a chair, Devon tried to let the admission make him feel better, but he couldn't shake the bitterness that his father and Bryce had kept him in the dark on this. It hurt not to be trusted, no matter what the reason. They should have known they could trust him, and worse yet, they should have known he would have eventually uncovered the truth. Did everyone truly think he was that big a fool?

"Todd's refusing to get help, can you believe it? He doesn't see that he's got a problem."

"I'll be keeping a rein on Todd's access to money."

"He needs rehab."

William held up a hand. "Now, Devon, let's not go that far. Todd got carried away, but making more out of it than necessary won't help anyone."

Devon's jaw dropped. "I can't believe you don't agree he needs professional help. This isn't a few thousand lost at the roulette wheel. He got himself in serious trouble and considering the denial he's in, he's going to end up doing it again."

"We can't just dump him in rehab. We've got to be sensitive to the image of this company."

"The company?"

"We're in the business of handling people's money. It'll be tricky enough rectifying the problems with this audit, we don't need the extra publicity of one of our executives admitting to a gambling problem."

"This is Todd's life we're talking about."

"And his needs have to be balanced with the needs of the company."

Devon leaned against the back of his chair, still not believing his ears. No wonder Todd was taking the matter so lightly. Their father intended to simply bail him out and shove the whole thing under the rug.

"He needs help, Dad."

"And after everything quiets down, we'll get him that help, but we have to take care of first things first. In the meantime, I'm tightening down on everything."

"Like taking away all our expense authority."

William looked apologetic. "I couldn't take away Todd's alone. It would have pointed the finger at him in the eyes of the auditors. It was easier to explain that I'd cut off everyone until we could properly back-up the transactions. When the time is right, I'll be restoring your authority." Smiling assuredly, he added, "Trust me. This will all work out and everything will be fine."

Spoken like a man talking to a four-year-old, Devon thought. His father had obviously come up with a plan of his own and intended to work things out the way he saw fit, be damned with what Devon thought or how he might want to approach the problem. If Devon hadn't wanted out of the firm before, he most certainly wanted out now. Not only would this job never be his fully, he now realized his father didn't even value his input or trust him with sensitive information.

What else was going on around here that Devon

didn't know about? How many other skeletons did the family have in the closet? Given this situation, he could only imagine what else went on behind his back.

It was a shot to his faith and his belief in what it meant to be a family. And more importantly, it was his final assurance that his future was not here at Bradshaw Investment Group.

"Well, you and Bryce can continue to work this out without me. I'm stepping down."

William sighed, not looking nearly as surprised as Devon expected, though he supposed lately he hadn't been secretive about his intentions.

"I wish you'd reconsider."

"Dad, you know this isn't a spur-of-the-moment decision. Face it, you aren't ready to give up control of this company and I like to do things my way. I can stick around and let this ruin our relationship or I can make the move we both know I need to make."

He studied his father, saw the reluctant acceptance in the man's eyes and a weight lifted from his shoulders. He hadn't wanted to put more stress on the man, but now he knew the stress would come from staying. Truth be told, he and his father were too much alike, two men insistent on running the ship with widely different ideas on how it should be done and that right there was a recipe for disaster. It was time one of them cut loose.

Devon added, "If you'd like to square this

mess away with Todd before making an announcement, that's fine with me. I don't have any immediate plans."

Then he turned and walked out feeling as though every problem in his life had now evaporated into thin air.

Every problem but one.

NICOLE READ THE SAME paragraph over three times before throwing down the article and admitting defeat. She'd come into the office early wanting to catch up on work in the hope of taking a couple days off, but she simply couldn't focus. Since seeing Devon three days ago she'd grown more and more dismayed, torn between feeling she needed some time to herself and the idea that maybe she didn't have to work through her problems alone. Granted, back in California, so many people had known about her adoption it had gotten chaotic. Here in Atlanta, Eve and Devon were the only two who knew the truth, and while at first it had been refreshing to get away from the clamor, she now found herself missing having someone to talk to about it.

She thought about Devon and the last time she'd seen him, and though she'd picked up the phone and nearly called a dozen times, she kept hanging up, deciding to take a few more days to think things through. She missed him more than she realized, her feelings for him stronger than she'd cared to admit, but fear kept her from acting on it, still uncertain whether she was ready for everything he wanted to give her.

So she'd decided to catch up at the office then take some time off work, a few days, maybe a week. She'd considered making a trip back home to see her friends and family or simply spending some time alone making solid decisions on what to do with her future.

And if she could just get through this article and leave this final portfolio for Penny, she could do exactly that. Unfortunately, she hadn't been able to keep her thoughts straight since she'd shown up this morning, and a ruckus outside wasn't helping.

What was it this time? she wondered. This part of Atlanta wasn't foreign to the occasional group of protestors or celebrity seekers. There were a number of television stations in Midtown, and on occasion, when word got out someone famous might be showing up for a guest appearance, crowds tended to gather.

She was about to get up from her desk to take a look when Eve popped in her doorway. Instead of speaking, she simply opened her mouth and pointed toward the window.

"Yes?" Nicole asked.

"Uh…have you been down there?"

"Down where?"

"The reporters," Eve started, and when she saw Nicole had no idea what she was talking about, she stepped into the office.

"Your adoption, Nicole. I don't know how—" she raised her hands to her sides. "I promise you it didn't come from me. But somehow Stella Graves got wind of your adoption. She's all but told everyone in Georgia you're looking for your birth parents and that a lucky family out there is related to a multi-millionaire."

"What?"

"All kinds of people are downstairs claiming to be related to you. I've already called Jenna. She'll be here any minute. Meanwhile, reporters are already here interviewing people. It's a mess, Nicky."

Needing to see for herself, she rushed over to the window that faced the front entrance of the building. Looking down from the second-story, she saw more than a dozen people standing in front of the station doors, some talking to press, others talking amongst themselves.

"Oh great," Nicole muttered, then moved to another window where she could get a better look at the crowd. The bulk of those talking to reporters couldn't possibly be related to her. They looked nothing like her.

She'd always expected her birth parents to be tall, fair and slender, like her, but these people spanned all different shapes, races and sizes. It was a wonder half of them could even think they were related.

A short woman with olive skin and jet black hair was being interviewed by a reporter, holding up what might be a picture to the camera. Nicole fought the urge to run down and confront her right then and there, certain the woman was a fraud.

But what if she wasn't?

What if she, or any of the other people in the crowd, really were her relations? This was what she'd wanted, wasn't it? She'd wanted to find her birth parents, to uncover where she'd come from, what kind of family she'd been born from. She wanted answers, the missing pieces of the puzzle put together so she could move on with her life feeling complete again.

What if this lottery could uncover the truth to her past? Why not turn this into a positive?

She studied the crowd, her hands trembling at the thought that any of these people might be her birth parents or know who her birth parents were. She didn't feel ready to find out, but at the same time, she couldn't live in this perpetual uncertainty forever. Maybe this was Fate stepping in and forcing forward motion.

Backing away from the window she returned to her desk, the image of the crowd adding a level of reality she hadn't dealt with before. She'd conjured up all kinds of fantasies, how they'd react to her and what kind of story they'd have to tell.

Her rational side knew anything was possible, including disappointment, but she'd always assumed even uncovering the worst was better than not knowing at all.

But now she began to think twice. Maybe like

many had said, she'd be better off not knowing than unearthing something ugly, and though she hadn't thought of it before now, she did have the money to consider. Did she really want to meet a family only interested in her because of her wealth? She had to face that possibility. She had to face *all* possibilities.

Like Devon had said, she could end up not liking what she found, and though she'd always known it, up until now, she hadn't truly faced it.

Eve took a seat at Nicole's desk. "I'm sorry, Nicky. Are you going to be okay?"

Nicole nodded. "I'm fine. It's that I hadn't expected this."

"Tell me about it. I just went through them all on my way in the door. You should see some of them. They're holding up baby pictures all claiming some sort of relation to you. One woman brought a baby blanket she said was yours and it still had the price tag on it!" Eve looked at her and sighed. "I'm so sorry, hon. I know this is the last thing you need right now."

Nicole held up a hand. "No, I'll be all right. In fact, in a way I'm glad this happened." When Eve flashed her a wide-eyed stare, Nicole explained, "I needed to make some sort of move when it came to this adoption thing. Maybe this is it."

Eve nodded in understanding and the two women chatted until a pretty African-American woman poked her head in the doorway and Nicole realized it was Jenna.

Nicole stood and accepted the handshake. "Thanks for coming."

Surrendering her seat to Jenna, Eve left the two women alone and Nicole explained the situation. Eve had already briefed Jenna when she'd called, but Nicole went through the details while Jenna took notes on a yellow legal pad.

After giving Jenna a chance to review her notes, Nicole asked, "So, what do we do about this?"

"We can handle it a couple ways," Jenna began. "It depends on how serious you are about finding your biological parents."

She looked up at Nicole as if waiting for an answer, but Nicole could only shrug. "I've been on the fence about it for a while now."

Jenna's smile was warm. "That's understandable."

"What are my options?"

Jenna set her pen down and relaxed in her chair. "We can hope that in a day or two this all goes away. Or we can sort through all these claims and see if any have merit. If you tell me what you know about your birth, we can discount any claim that's obviously false and send the impostors on their way. I would expect any valid relation would be able to answer some specific questions. Everyone else can be scared away by a few legal threats. But the point being, if we give people a place to go besides you, our office can handle this without the obvious emotional strings they'll try and hit you with."

She studied Nicole then added, "A little information off the Internet can sometimes sound very convincing. There's a lot of money involved here, money that people will try to bilk you out of claiming to be long-lost relatives. You need to be careful."

"So if I tell you what I do know, what happens if someone has a claim that appears valid? What do we do?"

"That will be up to you. Obviously, you realize the odds are incredibly slim any of these people are actually related to you. The more you know about your birth the more people we can weed out, but if someone should say all the right things—" she shrugged "—maybe this will be the end of your search."

The end of her search, but the beginning of what?

She stared at Jenna, wishing the woman could tell her what to do, but knowing this had to be her decision and only hers. She'd come to Atlanta seeking answers. This could be the way to get them. Had she been serious about finding her birth family or not? Taking a deep breath, she answered the question.

"Okay," she said. "Let's set up a hotline and screen these people. If my birth parents are really in that crowd, let's find them."

13

DEVON STARED at three identical cherrywood boards, trying to figure out why the assembly instructions for his new office unit considered them unique. They were exact replicas of each other, but damned if the diagram didn't clearly label them A, B and C as if one couldn't be substituted for the other.

For what seemed like forever, he stood alternately glancing from the pages to the boards, growing more and more convinced that someone at the factory had screwed up. If there was one solitary difference between these three slats of wood, he'd eat this instruction manual.

"No matter how long you stare at that thing, it's not going to assemble itself," Bryce said, shoving the discarded plastic sheeting and Styrofoam separators into one of the empty boxes.

"These boards are supposed to be different. How am I supposed to put the Number 3 pegs into Board A if I can't figure out which board is Board A?"

"Are you sure all the pegs aren't the same?"

"Yes, I am," Devon said, setting the pages down

on his old desk unit and holding up two plastic pegs. "One's longer than the other."

Bryce picked up the diagram and stepped over to the wall where Devon had leaned the three identical boards, looking over them with intent before pointing to the one on the left. "That's Board A."

Devon huffed. "How did you figure that out?"

"The holes on the edges of this one are about an inch closer to the center than the other two." He pointed to the diagram. "See this? That's definitely Board A."

Devon still didn't see it, but he wasn't going to argue. He now understood why the store charged two hundred dollars to assemble this thing. This was officially the last time he'd consider an assembly fee a rip-off. Standing there staring at a room littered with pegs, screws, boards and plastic things that could only be described as *diddly-bobs,* that two hundred dollars was beginning to look like a bargain, especially considering neither he nor Bryce were good at this sort of thing. Unless one of them had developed a keen sense of mechanical reasoning in the last few years, Devon was screwed.

"This is going to take all night," he complained.

"Tomorrow's another day."

"I've got plans tomorrow and Tuesday I'd wanted to get over to Computer Universe to order a new PC. I need this done today."

Bryce tossed a plastic bag full of scary-looking metal *do-dads* on the desk. "For a guy without a job, you sound awfully busy. What's with the tight schedule? You got a season of *X Files* reruns to get to?"

"For your information, I'm meeting Doug Petersen tomorrow on the very subject of jobs."

"Petersen Contracting?"

"Yup," Devon said, writing the letter A on a piece of masking tape and sticking it to the board Bryce had pointed to. He labeled the others as well, then stacked them in the corner to make room for the next pile of wood panels.

"What are you going to do, become a carpenter?" Bryce asked, completely tongue-in-cheek.

"Would that bother you?"

"Given how skillfully you're putting this desk unit together, I'd suggest you reconsider. The kid at the store would have had this and three like it done by now."

Devon half laughed. "Well, I'm not thinking carpenter, but I do want to talk to Doug about the contracting business in general."

Picking up what looked like a stack of matching shelves, he uncovered yet another plastic bag of hardware. "How can we have so much stuff and only four pages of instructions?"

Bryce flipped through the manual. "I don't know, but it's all here. The last page shows a fully assembled corner desk unit."

The two men worked, sorting through the pieces, making sure everything was there and organized, ready for assembly.

"So what *are* you going to do?" Bryce asked as he counted out screws and separated them into piles.

"I haven't decided yet, but whatever it is, it will be on *my* terms the way *I* want it."

Bryce glanced over, his tone sober. "You and Dad okay?"

Devon chuckled. "Honestly, I don't remember getting along with him better. I think he finally admitted to himself that I've been right all along." He paused, then added, "There's an ease between us that hasn't been there since I was a kid."

Bryce nodded. "Things have calmed down around the office now that the audit was squared away. Did Dad tell you about Todd?"

Devon was about to tack a numbered label on one board but stopped. "What about Todd?"

"He attended his first Gamblers Anonymous meeting night before last."

Devon's jaw went slack. "No way," he said, certain Bryce was pulling his leg. Todd had been so far from even acknowledging he had a problem, getting help should have been ages off.

Bryce raised a brow and smiled knowingly. "He didn't have a choice. Dad threatened to press charges for embezzlement if he didn't admit he was out of control."

"Well, good for the old man."

"You know he never would have turned him in."

"Probably, but I'd doubt that enough to give in if it had been me."

"As did Todd."

Ripping open a plastic bag of small screws and dumping them on the table, Bryce continued sorting. "I'd wanted to tell you what was going on, you know. It wasn't that we didn't trust you. It's that we all could have been indicted if this audit had turned out badly. Dad was trying to protect us, that's all."

Bryce didn't have to explain. After Devon had simmered down, he'd figured it out on his own, admitting he would have done the same thing if he'd been in their shoes. There hadn't been much he could have done to help, and knowing that Todd had been siphoning money off the books would have only put Devon on the hot seat with the rest of them.

"We're cool," he said. "It's *all* cool." Stepping out of the room to grab a couple beers, he returned and handed one to his brother. "This business of working with family was never for me, anyway. I've spent the last three years hanging around waiting for Dad to step down when really he's too young for retirement. It's time I took control of my life."

"Well, I've got to hand it to you. It would have been easy to just go along and take the job that was handed to you."

Devon shook his head. "I can't take a paycheck I'm not earning. This whole experience showed me very clearly who's really needed at the firm and who isn't. That's your job, Bryce. It's what you were meant to do, and I can't help but feel even Dad knew that, but feared saying so to spare my feelings." He twisted off the cap of his beer and took a swig. "And now that everyone's been honest with each other, I can finally move on with my life and figure out what *I* was meant to do."

"And will that new life include Nicole?"

Devon shrugged. "I wish I knew. Gracie had told me to give Nicole some space, and I've finally come around to agreeing." He slipped into a chair and stared at nothing in particular. "Unfortunately, I found the right girl at the wrong time, but maybe this is all for the best. I've got my own career to figure out then get off the ground. Maybe this is the wrong time for me, too." Though saying the words out loud didn't convince him. Part of him still felt he and Nicole could work through all this together, but until she agreed, it wasn't going to happen.

"Mom would say things happen for a reason."

"Yeah," Devon said absently. He hadn't missed the irony that all these weeks, Nicole had been trying to express her sense of betrayal over her parents' lies, how deep those wounds ran and how it wasn't something she could just shut off like a switch. As much as he tried, he hadn't truly understood, but this incident with Todd changed all that. Though things had turned out in the end, a side of him still reeled over the fact that his own brother had stolen from him and their family business.

Trying to remember it was the illness of addiction and not the man helped some, but he had to admit the sour feeling wasn't something that could be simply turned off.

This was something he and Todd would have to work through in their own time, just as Nicole had to work through her issues with her parents. If he'd learned anything, it was that resolution couldn't be forced or talked away with a simple quip or phrase. It had to be peeled away over time, layer by fragile layer.

As much as he wanted to stay a part of Nicole's life, she apparently needed to do this on her own, so he had no choice but to give her space.

"You're doing the right thing," Bryce said. "Give it some time, and if this thing is real between you two, it'll work out in the end."

NICOLE STOOD in front of aisles of computer hardware trying to remember the recommendations Nate had given her. She needed an upgraded laptop, and though she remembered the brand Nate had recommended, she now realized it might have been a good idea to write down the specifics. Standing here, with so many brands and options in front of her, everything looked the same, and she wondered if maybe she should hold off buying one until she went back home. Her father's birthday was a couple of weeks off, and she'd decided that would be a good time to make a trip to California for an extended weekend. After the initial publicity surrounding her adoption had died down, things had begun to calm, Jenna's hotline doing wonders in keeping the public at bay.

For the first time since she'd moved here, she felt as if she was making progress, that things were moving on the right course, and it was a welcome respite from the inner turbulence she'd been living with for over a year. She'd finally begun to feel relaxed. In fact, she could honestly say she almost felt happy.

Almost.

Still hanging over her head was the way she'd left things with Devon, him finding the file on her desk then storming out. She hadn't wanted to leave things on that note, had been tempted to call and iron it out, but feared the message it might send. Her feelings for him still raw, she didn't want to unintentionally pull him near while at the same time push him away. It wasn't fair to him, and though she ached to make things right, the mixed message a call might give wasn't worth the risk.

She needed to follow this new path and see where it took her, and only then could she consider opening her life to a lover. Her head said she had no other choice.

If only her heart would agree.

"Can I help you find something?"

She looked up to see the tall, heavy-set salesman who had been helping another couple a moment ago.

"Uh, yes, thank you." Blinking, she looked over the monstrous wall of electronics and said, "I'm looking to upgrade my laptop." Pointing to the brand her brother recommended, she added, "I'm considering these, but could use a recommendation on which one you think is best."

"The faster the better," came a smooth, familiar voice from behind her. She didn't need to turn and see who it was. The silky tingle down her spine told her it was Devon.

Spinning around, the sight of him reminded her of how this had all started. He looked good. Really good. A smoky gray T-shirt played up the blue in his eyes and the soft, worn jeans gave him that casual feel she loved so much. His quirked, half smile settled somewhere deep in her gut, stirring up feelings she hadn't yet buried, and her body responded with a mix of thrill and dread.

Glancing back at the salesman, she asked, "Can I catch up with you later?"

The man looked alternately at her and Devon then raised a hand and said, "Not a problem. Let me know when you're ready," before leaving the two alone.

"So, uh…how are you?" she asked, but she didn't need an answer. She could tell by looking at him life was going well. He looked calm and relaxed, like he hadn't a care in the world, and she couldn't help but feel their break-up had something to do with that.

"I'm doing good." Motioning behind him, he

added, "I'm setting up a bigger home office, so I'm on a shopping spree." Grinning, he added, "Computers and electronics—my favorite kind of shopping."

She giggled, but the clench on her throat combined with her nerves to make the laugh sound like something from a gawky school girl. She attempted to smooth it out by clearing her throat.

"A new home office?" she muttered.

His smile faded and he casually shrugged. "I'm officially self-employed."

Her jaw dropped. "You quit the firm?"

He nodded.

"Good for you! I mean…is it?"

He chuckled in that smooth, easy way that had caught her attention that night at the auction. The sweet genuine laugh had brought flutters to her stomach at the time, and still did today.

Apparently, her feelings for him were rawer than she'd expected.

"It is good," he said. "I'm going into business for myself, giving real estate a try. I'm having to go back to school to get my broker's license, but I'm looking forward to it. It feels right."

"Will you be selling homes?"

"Build them, preferably." Shoving a hand in his pocket, he smiled, but this time it didn't quite reach his eyes. "I've been thinking about our conversation…about your lottery winnings and doing something for the working class who could use a little help. I'm considering venturing into urban renewal, revitalizing old neighborhoods, developing affordable housing, things like that."

"I love that idea. You know, we still don't know what's happening with this lawsuit, but if things work out, maybe we could talk about funding some projects."

His smile deepened. "I'd like that."

For a moment, they stood, an uncomfortable silence settling between them, speaking to the many things that needed to be said but neither of them dared. Nicole felt the urge to explain herself once more, but knew she'd already done so probably more times than he cared to hear it. Yet she sensed Devon was holding his tongue, a flood of sentiments brimming under the surface ready to burst forth with the slightest prompting.

But she didn't prompt.

His life was facing the same turnabout as hers, both of them opening doors to an uncertain future. This simple fact that they'd made such progress in the short week they'd been apart confirmed this separation had been the smart move, and no matter how badly she ached to get back in his arms, she had to accept they'd acted wisely.

"I'd heard that your adoption made the papers." Lowering his voice, he added, "I'm sorry. How are you dealing with it?"

She forced a smile. "Actually, it ended up helping. I'm actively pursuing finding my birth parents with the help of Jenna Hamilton. She's the lawyer we hired to handle the suit, and she's doing a great job on both ends. We're talking about how to break through some of the confidentiality that surrounds sealed adoptions."

He nodded, his face displaying that same sense of reluctance he had every time she suggested seeking out her birth family.

"You think it's a mistake, don't you?" she asked.

He jerked and shook his head. "No, not at all. I think any move will be a move in the right direction."

"But seeking out my birth parents wouldn't have been your choice."

He let out a breath and dropped his shoulders. "Nicole, this isn't my choice. It's yours. And if you feel finding your birth family is the way to uncover your answers, then I think that's great."

Crossing her arms over her chest, she felt put off. She knew what he was saying between the lines, that he feared finding her birth family would create more problems than it solved, but he didn't understand.

"Devon, I can only resolve things by seeking them out. Leaving it all alone is just leaving it unresolved."

"If you've explored all your options and this is what you've chosen, I think you're doing the right thing."

She frowned. "What's that supposed to mean?"

Shaking his head, he huffed. "It means what I said. If you feel this is the way to get answers, I think that's wonderful. Progress is what counts, not the path you choose to get there."

Though his words sounded supportive, she couldn't shake the feeling that in some way, he was insinuating that finding her parents was an ignorant move.

And it solidified for her she'd made the wise move in breaking it off. She'd only recently found peace with her decision, and in one chance encounter with Devon, he'd managed to snatch it all away. This was precisely the internal debate she didn't need, and though it crushed her to admit it, she now saw they had no business being together at this point in their lives.

"I have made progress," she proclaimed. "And I intend to keep moving forward with it."

He nodded his consent and smiled. "That's great."

"It is," she confirmed, and not wanting to discuss it further, she added, "I should get back to my shopping. I'm only here on my lunch break and don't have much time."

His smile faded. "Okay, then."

Standing there for a brief moment, he opened his mouth as if to say something more, then simply added, "Be happy, Nicole. Okay?"

Jutting her chin, she replied, "I am."

But as she watched him disappear through the store, she felt anything but.

"WHY CAN'T I MAKE a decision and feel good about it?"

Nicole hadn't expected the statement to come

out in such a whine. It was just that she'd grown officially sick and tired of feeling confused and frustrated. It seemed every moment she made some sort of progress with her life, someone was there yanking it back, the latest being Devon and their chance meeting at the electronics warehouse.

After spending the day unable to focus on work, she'd grabbed Eve for an after-hours drink at Latitude 33, the local watering hole the crew often sought out after a particularly stressful week. And for Nicole, if this week didn't rank, nothing did.

Since running into Devon, she couldn't shake the sinking feeling in her gut that she'd gone off half-cocked, jumped all over the poor man when he was only trying to be nice. And the little voice in her head kept asking her why.

Why had she come off so defensive? Why had it taken barely an utterance from Devon to unravel everything she thought she'd accomplished?

"Maybe it's because you haven't made the right decision," Eve said, the comment echoing that voice Nicole had been trying to ignore.

Taking a sip of her wine, she fell back in her seat. "I thought I knew what I was doing, but after talking to Devon it doesn't work anymore. And the stupid thing is he didn't even try to tell me what to do."

More than once, she'd run the conversation over in her head, and every time, she came to the same conclusion. He was the one person in her life she couldn't avoid being honest with. She could con everyone else into believing she knew what she was doing, but Devon could see through her, staring back at her like a mirror that showed only the truth. He didn't even have to express himself with words. She'd felt it simply by stating her intentions to him, that unsettled feeling that the line she was feeding him didn't hold water.

And no matter how badly she tried to shake it off, she couldn't. When she really looked into that mirror of truth, she saw he'd been on the mark about everything. She *was* angry with her parents. And a part of her *had* moved here to Atlanta to punish them. Sure, she'd needed to get away and clear her head, but she hadn't needed to settle here and she certainly hadn't needed to pack up her whole life and start over again.

That had been her childish side reacting, and of all the people who had offered their opinions and advice, Devon had been the only one to see through it all and tell it to her straight. And though it hurt to admit it, damn, if he hadn't been right.

A small crowd at the bar cheered, and the two women glanced over to see them staring at a broadcast of the day's Braves game.

The sight left her melancholy.

"Are you having second thoughts about finding your birth parents?"

"I'm having second thoughts about everything." Staring closely at Eve, she added, "Before I knew I was adopted, I was happy. I felt blessed. I have a great family, and here I am looking for something else. And for what? Because I think it will take the hurt away?" She took a large gulp of her wine then set the glass down. "What am I hoping to gain? Do I care why my birth parents gave me up? Not really. Do I want to see what they look like, find out if I have any other siblings?" She shook her head. "You know, I definitely understand how other people would have those questions, but in all the shock and turmoil, I've never once cared about any of that. Not in any real sense."

"Then why are you looking?"

Nicole shook her head. "Because I thought I should. And I think a side of me thought meeting my birth parents would give me someone else to be angry with besides my parents." Unwanted tears welling in her eyes, she confessed, "I'm so angry with them, but I don't want to be. I want to let all this go. I love my family. And they love me, that's all that matters. I guess I thought if I had strangers to focus my anger on, the rest of my life would come back to me."

"That seems logical, but I think you'd find out in the long run it doesn't work like that."

"No, it doesn't. And Devon knew it. How could someone walk in and flat-out tell it like it is when dozens of people before him—including paid therapists—couldn't?"

"I don't know," Eve said, and then she smiled. "Maybe he's special."

"He *is* special. And in more ways than just knowing me and my troubles."

"So have you called to tell him that?"

Nicole opened her mouth to answer but was interrupted by her cell phone. She pulled it from her purse, and when the caller ID showed it was Jenna Hamilton, she quickly flipped it open. "Hello?"

"Nicole, it's Jenna. I have good news." The tone in Jenna's voice caused her pulse to quicken. "One of the women who called our office about your adoption appears to have answered all the questions correctly."

"Really?"

"It's no guarantee she's your birth mother, but I think there's enough promise in what she's said that you might want to talk to her."

Nicole's heart skipped a beat. This was supposedly what she'd come to Atlanta for, but now that the reality was within her grasp she didn't know anymore. What she'd wanted was to find her family—ignoring the fact that she already had one—and one who loved her and accepted her. And never gave her a moment's doubt about who she was or to whom she belonged.

She'd wanted to feel normal again, to stop doubting who she was and to find her ability to trust again. And none of those things were going to happen by meeting some woman who gave birth to her and didn't want her to know her identity.

Sitting there with Eve, it all suddenly became clear. There was a reason she'd been here nearly a year without making any real progress toward finding her family. She didn't want another family. Yes, she was angry with her parents, had wished they'd told her from the start, but when she really dug down deep, she knew Devon had spoken the truth. Finding out about her adoption didn't change who she was. She'd only felt it should have, and her hurt and anger prevented her from seeing that.

Truth was she liked who she was. She liked her parents, her family, her brother and her life. They'd all raised her to be a Reavis, and blood or no blood, that's exactly who she was.

And in that moment, she felt the freedom of a life that finally made sense, and without the slightest reluctance, she responded to Jenna and said, "No, thanks."

"No?"

"No. My adoption records are sealed, and that's the way I want them to stay. My parents are Don and Betty Reavis. Whoever gave birth to me is just that and I'd like to keep it that way."

"Nicole, you can think this over. You don't have to decide immediately."

She looked to Eve, who responded with a wide encouraging grin, and she felt as though months of angst and turmoil had fallen from her shoulders. "I don't need to reconsider. The tabloids were wrong. I didn't come to Atlanta to find my birth parents. I've already got a family back in California, and it's all the family I need."

"You're sure you won't change your mind."

"Tell her and any others, thanks but no thanks."

Flipping the phone closed, she turned to Eve and asked, "What was that you said about feeling good about a decision?"

"Uh, something about feeling good when you've made the right one."

Nicole nodded. "*This* was the right decision."

14

Please join me for a
private celebration
Place: Santiago Resort and Spa
Time: Saturday, five p.m. sharp!
Room 182
P.S. Bring Gabe

DEVON TUCKED THE RED scented card in his pocket as he made his way down the corridor toward the hotel room, curious to see what his mystery host had in store for him. Not that the identity of the sender was much of a mystery. Though the card hadn't been signed and had been hand-delivered by his nine-year-old neighbor who'd been given five dollars to keep quiet about where he got it, the attached get-out-of-jail-free card stapled under the post script gave it away.

He only wondered what Nicole had in mind, and why she'd drawn him to the resort that would have been their first date had she won the bidding at the Children's Charity auction.

After seeing her last week, he didn't think he'd

ever hear from her again. For the first time since trouble began brewing between them, he truly felt they'd said their goodbyes. She'd looked good, like she was finally starting to work through her issues. And it seemed as if her new life wouldn't be including him.

He'd told himself to move on, to leave the next move to her, and after nearly a week, he'd all but conceded there wouldn't be a next move. Until he stepped out of the house to find his neighbor, Trenton, standing on the porch with the red card in his hand.

And five p.m. couldn't come soon enough.

He had no idea where she was going with this; whether she was only looking for a weekend fling or something more, he hadn't a clue and didn't care. Given everything she was going through, he'd resolved not to push, so at least until her life calmed down, he'd be satisfied with however casually she wanted to play this.

Coming to the end of the corridor, room 182 was the final doorway on his right, and with much anticipation, he held up a fist and gently knocked. It took a few seconds before he heard the footsteps and the click of the door, and then he was greeted with the brightest, most beautiful smile he'd seen in weeks.

"You came," she said, pulling back the door and making room for him to pass.

"Did you think I wouldn't?"

Closing the door behind them, she admitted, "After the way we left things, I feared you might not."

Apparently, she wasn't quite clear just how hard he'd fallen for her, so he decided to show her. Cupping her cheek in his hand, he backed her against the door and pressed his lips to hers, his excitement welling when she all but melted in his arms. She tasted of dry wine and smelled like sunshine, and when she moaned invitingly and pulled him closer, his body yearned for its mate.

Her snug, silky dress felt good in his hands, like satin sheets against bare skin, and when he migrated his lips down the nape of her neck, her chuckle tickled his ear.

"You're insufferable," she said.

"I've missed you."

"You don't even know why you're here yet."

"It's not for this?"

Wiggling away from him, she took his hand and led him into the room. "There are things I have to tell you first."

The large suite had been lit with dozens of candles casting a yellow glow over the dark green and burgundy room. Out on the private balcony, an oversized spa bubbled and hissed. Next to it stood a tray of chocolate-dipped strawberries and other fruits and pastries. The king size bed had been turned down and he smiled when he noticed all three parts of The Godfather sitting near the television.

She'd obviously planned a night of sex and romance, and when she poured them both a glass of champagne and took a seat on the couch, he didn't hesitate to join her.

Handing him his glass, she tipped it to hers and toasted, "To new beginnings."

"New beginnings," he said, not quite sure what exactly was beginning.

Scooting closer, she explained, "Today, I'm starting my life over again."

"Today," he said.

"Yep. I'm reclaiming the person I was. Before this adoption turned me on my head."

Though her face displayed pure delight, he had to wonder where this was heading.

"That's a good thing, right?" he asked, meaning was it good for *them?*

She winked. "I don't know. The old Nicole was a little bossy and pretty opinionated. And when she wanted something, she took it, be damned with the consequences. That and she could be impulsive, especially when it came to shoes."

He wanted to say he could live with that, but wasn't certain she was asking.

Setting her champagne on the side table, she moved in closer and placed a slim hand on his chest. "I've decided not to seek out my birth parents. I realized there was a lot of truth in what you said. Before I found out about this adoption, I'd been happy. I'd had just about everything I'd wanted in life, including a family that loved me." Shaking her head, she admitted, "That's what I need. That's all

I need. Oh, that and one other thing." Taking the champagne from his hand, she set it on the table and moved into his arms. "You see, before I can move forward with my life, I need to go back and fix some things I screwed up."

He raised a brow. "Such as?"

"Such as that bachelor auction and that romantic date I let slip away."

He brushed a hand down her hair, caressing the golden strands between his fingers. "That explains the invitation."

"You said something about dinner, a spa, maybe some golf, and with the right woman, who knows what else."

"I'd call you the right woman."

Her smile warmed him, and thoughts of the next several hours left him anxious and excited.

Moving up on her knees, she leaned over and straddled him, wrapping her arms around his neck and pressing a light kiss to his lips. His hands found their way to her breasts, and his cock hardened when he realized she wasn't wearing a bra.

"Then there's all those things we'd wanted to get to when you took me up to The Point in Gabe," she whispered. "I have every intention of finishing what we started that night."

He tasted her lips. "I've got the get-out-of-jail-free card."

"Let's hope we don't need it."

He palmed her breasts through the silky fabric

of her dress, clutching the mounds in his hands and moving his lips down her chin toward the tender flesh below. Though a side of him begged to know where this was leading up to, her gifted fingers kept him locked in the moment. One by one, she popped open each shirt button until his chest was fully exposed. Then she went to work circling his nipples with her thumbs, caressing his pecs and raising the temperature in his veins a few thousand degrees. God, the woman could turn him on, and as she rocked over him, slowly grinding her hips against his jeans, his cock began to strain. He wondered how many times they'd have to make love before he could take her slow and easy. He'd thought they'd be here by now, but his every moment with her left him thirsting for release, starved and anxious as if he'd never been with a woman before.

With her breasts in his hands, her fingers gently stroked his hair, his shoulders, his back and that sweet ass humped pressure where it shouldn't. He needed to make a move before he climaxed right there on the couch.

"Hold on," he said, grabbing her waist and lifting from the couch. She wrapped her legs around him while he maneuvered over to the bed and tossed her down, a quick exhale rushing from her lungs. He pulled a condom from his pocket then yanked off his pants and pushed them aside.

"Much better." Lowering down, he brought her into his arms. Her silky dress cascaded over his thighs and he slid his hands up under the hem, groaning with pleasure when he discovered she wasn't wearing any underwear either. It was just her luscious body, draped in silken pleasure, and when he cupped a hand between her legs and felt the slick heat of desire, he groaned, "*Much* better."

He tugged one sleeve off her shoulder and began feasting on her breast, needing to find some semblance of control but coming up short every time. From the first moment they met, she'd reduced him to his most primal state, and though they'd made love countless times since then, she always managed to unravel him.

"Better," she said, "but not good enough." She wrapped a leg around his thigh and arched in closer, taking the condom from his hand and ripping open the package. "I've got more to tell you."

"I'm all ears," he said to her breast, tugging off the other sleeve and exposing both of the tender mounds. He placed his face between them and sucked in a breath, wanting to absorb her deepest essence. The woman was beauty from head to toe, her body picking up where her spirit left off, the two compounding into a package that drove him to the edge every time.

And tonight wouldn't be any different. Thirty seconds with her in his arms and his body ached for more, and he knew no matter what she had planned for this weekend, all the sex in the world wouldn't be enough.

Tucking the condom in his palm, she said, "I need you in me," and he wasn't going to argue. If there was anything he'd learned during the last month, his golden lover shared his thirst. It was just one of the many reasons he loved her.

Backing off the bed, he took her hand and pulled her into his arms then unzipped her dress, letting the fabric fall to the ground. For a moment, he stood and stared. Her cheeks had a rosy hue and her eyes displayed a depth he'd never seen before. Maybe it was the candlelight, maybe it was her decision to move on with her life releasing the hurt she'd been carrying around.

Right now, he wanted to show her how he felt, and after rolling on the condom, they kissed their way back to the bed and under the covers.

She moved under him and held his cock in her hands, hardening every muscle in his body and rushing more blood to his loins.

"Get inside," she urged, and he obeyed, lifting his hips and driving deep between her legs.

The air rushed from her lungs and she clasped a hand to the back of his neck and brought his mouth to hers, circling her tongue inside and sucking it in as if she were feeding on his very soul. He liked this greedy side of her, this demanding side that he'd come to love, and as he settled into the kiss, he began pumping them toward release.

"There's one more thing to tell you," she whispered to his mouth.

"Tell me," he urged.

Her breath drew short and she whispered, "That time you told me you loved me, I blew it."

"You didn't blow anything," he said, and it was true. He'd come on too strong too fast, and now that he had her back, he intended to take things as easy as she needed.

"Yes, I did." And as the sensation began to build, she added, "I should have told you I love you, too."

He stopped and looked carefully into her eyes.

"You what?"

The smile on her face said his ears hadn't betrayed him.

"I love you," she said. "And I'd like to start my new life with you in it."

He lifted up to his hands and hovered over her, wondering if this moment could be any sweeter.

"You love me."

"With everything I have."

Emotion welled in his chest and he pulled her into his arms, burying his face in the crook of her neck, wanting every inch of his body next to hers. "Oh, Nicole," he murmured, "I do love you."

"Now take me like it should be," she said, curving her back and spreading wider. "Make love to me. Real love."

He moved inside, bringing his lips to hers and drinking in the very essence of what she'd offered. Love. Real love. The kind that would bring them together and allow them to tackle the world. And between his family and hers, there would be a lot of tackling to do.

But something told him that together, they'd found the kind of bond that could make the little problems disappear and the big ones bearable. And in this world that's exactly what they needed.

Someone to count on.

Someone to believe in.

And bringing their bodies and souls to the edge and over, he knew that's exactly what they would be together.

"HOW DID YOU MANAGE access to this private road?" Devon asked from the backseat of Gabe. She passed him a sandwich and a bag of chips while he uncorked the wine and filled two plastic glasses.

"I found a romantic security guard with keys to the gate. But if we aren't back down the hill by nine o'clock, they're locking us up here."

He checked his watch. "That's plenty of time for everything I'd like to do."

She cast a curious look. "I thought we already did it."

"There's at least a half-dozen lovemaking positions to be explored in the back of this Caddy, and that's without even taking the top down."

She eyed their surroundings. "Hmm, I'm envisioning three interesting ones right now."

Devon grinned and unwrapped a sandwich from the goodies they'd picked up from room service before leaving the resort and heading for the foothills.

"And then we should take a moment or two to enjoy the view. I owe the guard a case of beer for this."

"I thought you said he was a romantic."

"He is. The beer's a cover so his coworkers won't ride him over it."

Devon laughed, and for the first time since they'd met, Nicole truly laughed with him.

Once Nicole had made the right decision, everything fell into place. The moment she'd told Jenna her search was over, she went home and called her parents, fleshing out once and for all her feelings of anger over why they did what they did, yet ultimately finding the forgiveness and understanding she'd sought. And when she'd finally been truthful about her feelings—hard as they were to express—it was as if her life clicked into place. She'd come to Atlanta to get answers, to resolve her issues, and that's exactly what she'd done.

Just not in the way she'd expected.

"I wanted to ask you," she said. "My father's birthday is coming up. I'm planning to go home for a long weekend and was hoping you'd come with me."

He smiled. "Meet the parents? This sounds serious."

"It is serious. And you need to impress them or my father won't give you permission to marry me."

Devon choked on his wine. "Marry you?"

She burst with laughter. "I'm kidding! Man, you should see the look on your face."

After clearing his throat, he shook his head and said, "Actually, I kind of like the sound of it."

"Meet my family first. They might pounce on you so fiercely you'll be hopping the next plane back to Georgia. I am their baby girl, you know."

"You survived my family. I think I can survive yours."

"Good point," she said, then set her sandwich aside, curled into his arms and pressed a kiss to his cheek.

He looked at her inquisitively. "What was that for?"

"For loving me when I was at my worst."

He kissed her back. "If that was your worst, our lives are going to be a piece of cake."

And with the sun setting behind the hills casting a pink haze over the evening sky, Nicole had to agree. She'd faced the most difficult time in her life and came out the other end stronger and more secure than she'd imagined. It had been true. She had needed to get away from California to see life more clearly, but what she'd also needed was the help of someone who saw her more clearly than she saw herself.

What once seemed like a life impossibly tattered now felt more whole and complete than it ever had before, and she knew with Devon on her side, they'd be able to face whatever the future had in store for them.

"I can't say I'm completely over this, but I've stopped doubting myself, and I've stopped doubting us," she said. "And since you've stuck with me this far, I'm confident we'll figure the rest out."

"Hmm, sounds like what I've been trying to tell you all along."

She smiled and kissed him again. "Are you expecting me to admit you told me so?"

"It wouldn't hurt."

"Neither would this," she said, moving the sandwich from his lap and unzipping his jeans.

"Are you trying to use sex to avoid admitting I was right?" he asked.

"Are you complaining?"

He began to protest, but when she grasped his cock in her hand and bent down for a taste, his only response was, "Not at all, babe. Not at all."

LIZA SKINNER picked up her latte and stepped toward the doors of the coffee shop when her cell phone rang. Setting the paper cup on a nearby table, she checked the number, her heart skipping a beat when she saw it was her lawyer, Kevin. She'd called him several times over the past two days, growing more and more concerned as time went without a call back.

She slipped into a chair and flipped open the phone.

"Tell me you've got good news," she said.

"I'm afraid I don't have any news." He sounded tired and a bit exasperated, but that was too bad. Yes, she'd been hounding him for updates, and yes, he'd said he'd call when he had something to tell her. But this lawsuit was a big deal to her and it had been over a week since he'd had anything concrete to tell her. Surely, in a week's time he'd have accomplished *something*.

"Have you done anything with this suit at all lately?"

"I've been working on nothing but," he defended. "But this isn't open and shut." Sighing, he added, "You need to brace yourself for the reality that this might not work out in your favor. If this suit goes to court, I don't know that you have a leg to stand on."

She balled her hand into a fist. "I don't need to brace myself for failure. What I need is a lawyer who won't let that happen. I've got to win this thing, and if you can't do that for me, tell me now so I can find someone who can."

"I haven't said you'll lose. I only said this isn't a sure thing."

"Well, find a way to make it one."

Slamming the phone shut, she eyed her coffee, realizing it was the last thing she needed right now. Her nerves were already wired and the call from Kevin hadn't helped. She knew she should have taken more time in selecting a lawyer. Unfortunately, time was at a premium these days. She needed her money and she needed it now.

* * * * *

Don't miss the next
MILLION DOLLAR SECRETS
THE NAKED TRUTH
by Shannon Hollis
Available next month!

Welcome to cowboy country...

Turn the page for a sneak preview of
TEXAS BABY
by
Kathleen O'Brien
An exciting new title from
Harlequin Superromance for everyone
who loves stories about the West.

Harlequin Superromance—
Where life and love weave together in
emotional and unforgettable ways.

CHAPTER ONE

CHASE TRANSFERRED his gaze to the road and identified a foreign spot on the horizon. A car. Almost half a mile away, where the straight, tree-lined drive met the public road. He could tell it was coming too fast, but judging the speed of a vehicle moving straight toward you was tricky.

It wasn't until it was about two hundred yards away that he realized the driver must be drunk...or crazy. Or both.

The guy was going maybe sixty. On a private drive, out here in ranch country, where kids or horses or tractors or stupid chickens might come darting out any minute, that was criminal. Chase straightened from his comfortable slouch and waved his hands.

"Slow down, you fool," he called out. He took the porch steps quickly and began walking fast down the driveway.

The car veered oddly, from one lane to another, then up onto the slight rise of the thick green spring grass. It just barely missed the fence.

"Slow down, damn it!"

He couldn't see the driver, and he didn't recognize this automobile. It was small and old, and couldn't have cost much even when it was new. It was probably white, but now it needed either a wash or a new paint job or both.

"Damn it, what's wrong with you?"

At the last minute, he had to jump away, because the idiot behind the wheel clearly wasn't going to turn to avoid a collision. He couldn't believe it. The car kept coming, finally slowing a little, but it was too late.

Still going about thirty miles an hour, it slammed into the large, white-brick pillar that marked the front boundaries of the house. The pillar wasn't going to give an inch, so the car had to. The front end folded up like a paper fan.

It seemed to take forever for the car to settle, as if the trauma happened in slow motion, reverberating from the front to the back of the car in ripples of destruction. The front windshield suddenly seemed to ice over with lethal bits of glassy frost. Then the side windows exploded.

The front driver's door wrenched open, as if the car wanted to expel its contents. Metal buckled hideously. Small pieces, like hubcaps and mirrors, skipped and ricocheted insanely across the oyster-shell driveway.

Finally, everything was still. Into the silence, a plume of steam shot up like a geyser, smelling of rust and heat. Its snake-like hiss almost smothered the low, agonized moan of the driver.

Chase's anger had disappeared. He didn't feel anything but a dull sense of disbelief. Things like this didn't happen in real life. Not in his life. Maybe the sun had actually put him to sleep....

But he was already kneeling beside the car. The driver was a woman. The frosty glass-ice of the windshield was dotted with small flecks of blood. She must have hit it with her head, because just below her hairline a red liquid was seeping out. He touched it. He tried to wipe it away before it reached her eyebrow, though, of course that made no sense at all. Her eyes were shut.

Was she conscious? Did he dare move her? Her dress was covered in glass, and the metal of the car was sticking out lethally in all the wrong places.

Then he remembered, with an intense relief, that every good medical man in the county was here, just behind the house, drinking his champagne. He found his phone and paged Trent.

The woman moaned again.

Alive, then. Thank God for that.

He saw Trent coming toward him, starting out at a lope, but quickly switching to a full run.

"Get Dr. Marchant," Chase called. "Don't bother with 911."

Trent didn't take long to assess the situation. A fraction of a second, and he began pulling out his cell phone and running toward the house.

The yelling seemed to have roused the woman.

She opened her eyes. They were blue and clouded with pain and confusion.

"Chase," she said.

His breath stalled. His head pulled back. "What?"

Her only answer was another moan, and he wondered if he had imagined the word. He reached around her and put his arm behind her shoulders. She was tiny. Probably petite by nature, but surely way too thin. He could feel her shoulder blades pushing against her skin, as fragile as the wishbone in a turkey.

She seemed to have passed out, so he put his other arm under her knees and lifted her out. He tried to avoid the jagged metal, but her skirt caught on a piece and the tearing sound seemed to wake her again.

"No," she said. "Please."

"I'm just trying to help," he said. "It's going to be all right."

She seemed profoundly distressed. She wriggled in his arms, and she was so weak, like a broken bird. It made him feel too big and brutish. And intrusive. As if touching her this way, his bare hands against the warm skin behind her knees, were somehow a transgression.

He wished he could be more delicate. But he smelled gasoline, and he knew it wasn't safe to leave her here.

Finally he heard the sound of voices, as guests began to run around the side of the house, alerted by Trent. Dr. Marchant was at the front, racing toward them as if he were forty instead of seventy. Susannah was right behind him, her green dress floating around her trim legs.

"Please," the woman in his arms murmured again. She looked at him, the expression in her blue eyes lost and bewildered. He wondered if she might be on drugs. Hitting her head on the windshield might account for this unfocused, glazed look, but it couldn't explain the crazy driving.

"Please, put me down. Susannah... The wedding..."

Chase's arms tightened instinctively, and he froze in his tracks. She whimpered, and he realized he might be hurting her. "Say that again?"

"The wedding. I have to stop it."

* * * * *

Be sure to look for TEXAS BABY,
available September 11, 2007,
as well as other fantastic Superromance titles
available in September.

Welcome to Cowboy Country...

TEXAS BABY

by Kathleen O'Brien

#1441

Chase Clayton doesn't know what to think.
A beautiful stranger has just crashed his
engagement party, demanding that he not
marry because she's pregnant with his baby.
But the kicker is—he's never seen her before.

Look for TEXAS BABY and other fantastic
Superromance titles on sale September 2007.

Available wherever books are sold.

HARLEQUIN *Super Romance*

**Where life and love weave together
in emotional and unforgettable ways.**

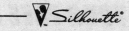

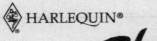

COMING NEXT MONTH

#345 KIDNAPPED! Jo Leigh
Forbidden Fantasies

She had a secret desire to be kidnapped and held against her will.... But when heiress Tate Baxter's fantasy game turns out to be all too real, can sexy bodyguard Michael Caulfield put aside his feelings and rescue her in time?

#346 MY SECRET LIFE Lori Wilde
The Martini Dares, Bk. 1

Kate Winfield's secrets were safe until hottie Liam James came along. Now the sexy bachelor with the broad chest and winning smile is insisting he wants to uncover the delectable Katie—from head to toe.

#347 OVEREXPOSED Leslie Kelly
The Bad Girls Club, Bk. 3

Isabella Natale works in the family bakery by day, but at night her velvet mask and G-string drive men wild. Her double life is a secret, even from Nick Santori, the club's hot new bodyguard who's always treated her like a kid. Now she's planning to show the man of her dreams that while it's okay to look, it's *much* better to touch....

#348 SWEPT AWAY Dawn Atkins
Sex on the Beach

Her plan was simple. Candy Calder would use her vacation to show her boss Matt Rockwell she was serious about her job. But her plan backfired when he invited her to enjoy the sinful side of Malibu. With an offer this tempting, what girl could refuse?

#349 SHIVER AND SPICE Kelley St. John
The Sexth Sense, Bk. 3

She's not alive. She's not dead. She's something in between. And medium Dax Vicknair wants her desperately! Dax fell madly in love with teacher Celeste Beauchamp when he helped one of her students cross over. He thought he was destined to live without her. But now Celeste is back—and Dax intends to make the most of their borrowed time....

#350 THE NAKED TRUTH Shannon Hollis
Million Dollar Secrets, Bk. 3

Risk taker Eve Best is on the verge of having everything she's ever wanted. But what she really wants is the handsome buttoned-down executive Mitchell Hayes, who must convince the gorgeous talk-show host to say "yes" to his business offer *and* his very private proposition....

www.eHarlequin.com

HBCNM0807